ELLIOTT HAY

#3 VIGILAUNTIE JUSTICE

I0708841

SWIPE RIGHT
FOR A BIT OF
MURDER

KNITTING. TEA. GOSSIP ... VENGEANCE

 Formatted with Vellum

**WHEN MR RIGHT TURNS OUT TO BE MR WRONG,
MURDER MIGHT BE THE ONLY OPTION...**

Baz, Peggy, Carole, and Madge may look like a quartet of average grans meeting up at the local café. But they're not above a bit of vengeance ... vigilauntie-style. And the streets of south-east London wouldn't be safe without them.

When the ladies get wind of a romance fraudster preying on innocent locals, their hearts sink. Scammers of this kind are usually overseas − beyond their unofficial jurisdiction.

But when more victims in their community come forward, it becomes apparent this fraudster may be closer than they suspected. And why does every clue they uncover lead back to themselves?

This time, they're dealing with a dangerous criminal not even the fastest mobility scooter can outrun. But as far as they're concerned, a bit of murder can solve anything...

content warnings

This work contains the following:

- Fraud and romance scams
- Transphobia and queerphobia

The *Vigilauntie Justice* books are cosy(ish) noir(ish) stories set in London. They do have on-page violence, including murder, but it's never graphic. There's no sex and minimal swearing and romance – but there's heaps of queer content and found family.

author's note

This book is written in British English. If you're used to reading American English, some of the spelling and punctuation may seem unusual. I promise, it's totally safe.

This story also features a number of Canadianisms. Sadly, I cannot promise these are safe. You may find yourself involuntarily wearing a touque and craving Timbits and a double-double. It can't be helped. Seek treatment immediately.

previously on vigilauntie justice...

Okay, you know how in TV shows you get that little one-minute segment at the start of each episode to catch you up? Books should do that too, I think. Just a handy little reminder since it may have been a while since you read the previous books. Or maybe you're like me and you've jumped right in at book three. No judgement.

Previously on *Vigilauntie Justice*... [You may want to imagine Anthony Stewart Head's voice as you read this.]

Baz is a newly divorced, newly retired, newly out trans woman. After having lived much of her life in Canada, she returns to south-east London. Her first task is to make some new friends.

She joins forces with three women who meet up every morning at a local café. Peggy is a septuagenarian punk and proud lesbian. Peggy's life partner, Carole, is a bit unusual ... in so many ways. Madge is a retired nurse, a social butterfly, and an eminently pragmatic woman.

But it turns out that her new friends aren't just crafters,

they're vigilantes. Vigilaunties, even. And now Baz is one of them.

CHAPTER 1

in which an unfortunate event befalls our heroine

BAZ STILL GOT palpitations every time she crossed here. After checking to make sure no one was turning south onto Brookmill Road, she steered her mobility scooter into the road, heading towards the café for her daily get-together with the girls.

Nine months earlier, she'd injured her left knee crossing this very road. It was a hard lesson to learn, but she knew better than to set out without looking to make sure that the drivers turning left knew they had a delayed signal.

It was a lovely summer morning. The sun was at her back and she was on her way to meet her friends.

Her right knee was doing well too. She could probably walk to the café without the scooter now. In fact, she might try just that one morning. But then – what would happen if she made it halfway and then ran out of steam? Or if the pain became unbearable?

No, maybe that wasn't such a good idea.

It had been fifteen months since the surgery to repair her right knee – and more than a year and a half since the life-changing injury that had ended her career with the RCMP. She'd taken early retirement and accepted the generous compensation won for her by the excellent solicitor at her husband's – *sorry, ex-husband's* – firm.

No, she wasn't going to start thinking about Hari or their life back in Canada. That wouldn't do. He'd made his feelings clear. He was happy for her. He understood that transitioning was right for her. But he was a gay man – Hari could never be with a woman.

And besides, she had Paul now. Didn't she?

Paul, who was so sweet and kind. They'd been seeing each other for four months – though they were still taking things slowly.

But Baz had been with Hari for thirty years. The idea of starting over with someone new still felt utterly alien to her.

Something slammed into her side. An involuntary scream tore from her. Wind whipped her hair. Fabric flapped in front of her face.

The whole thing was over in a flash, leaving her panting as she waited for her heart rate to fall back to normal levels. But she had no idea what had actually happened.

She hadn't even realised she'd stopped moving – though of course she had as soon as she let go of the scooter's accelerator – until a young man spoke. 'You all right, miss? Did they get anything?' He was holding her shoulder, propping her up on her left side.

His words weren't making any sense. *Nothing* made any sense.

She'd nearly fallen out of her scooter.

Clutching her throat, Baz tried to catch enough breath to respond. And to right herself so she was sitting upright without his support. 'Thank you, I'm fine, I think. They... What? Who?'

The young man – who was he? He stretched an arm out,

pointing down New Cross Road, towards central London. 'The thieves?'

Baz looked where he was indicating. Horns blared and people shouted at a motorbike as it squeezed between cars and ran the red at the bottom of Tanner's Hill. 'What?'

'Did they?' he repeated. He was tall and muscular, with long locs hanging over his deep brown skin. His bright blue polo shirt was tucked into his trousers, giving him access to the tool belt at his waist.

Baz's heart was still in her throat. 'Did who what, dear?'

'Did they get anything?' The young man bent and looked into her eyes, like he was trying to gauge her mental fitness – which she supposed he was.

'No, no,' she reassured him. 'I'm completely fine.' She made to lift her handbag to demonstrate her point ... only it wasn't there. 'Oh. Oh, no.'

He cocked his head sympathetically. 'Phone?'

She frowned. 'Afraid so. They grabbed my handbag – which had my phone and my wallet in it. And everything else. Oh dear.' She wasn't going to cry. Not here. Not now.

The man smiled kindly. 'Sorry, auntie. Can I ring somebody for you?'

Baz realised she was still clenching her fists and made a concerted effort to relax them. 'My friends.'

The young man pulled a phone from his pocket.

'No, sorry, dear. I mean, I'm on my way to meet them. At the café just ahead.' Baz waved a hand in the direction she'd been heading.

'Mrs Dixon's place – is that what you mean?'

Baz breathed slowly. Of course he knew Madge. Everyone knew Madge. 'Yes, Wellbeloved – that's the one.'

He nodded. 'C'mon. I'll walk you there. Make sure you're all right.'

'Thank you.' Baz turned the speed knob down then wrapped her fingers around the scooter's accelerator. She began to inch forwards. 'I appreciate your help. I hope I'm not keeping you from anything.'

'Nah, fam. My work can live without me for five minutes.' He walked alongside her as they made their way to the café.

'Oh? Where do you work?' It still took effort to prevent her voice from shaking.

He waved at the logo on his chest. 'Just over at the Wickes on Blackheath Road – you know it?'

'Oh dear.' Bile rose in Baz's throat as she realised her mistake. 'I've got you going the wrong direction.' Her emotions were all over the shop.

He flashed a thousand-watt grin at her. 'Nah, we're cool. It won't take long. Need to make sure you're a'right, innit? My mum would never forgive me if I didn't deliver you safely into the hands of your friends.'

'Here we are.' Baz steered her mobility scooter into its usual spot between the public car park and the outdoor tables at Wellbeloved Café. She switched the engine off and went to drop the keys into her handbag – before realising her error.

'Y'aright?' Her new friend had a concerned look on his face. He held out his elbow for her to take.

Baz smiled as she accepted his arm. 'I will be. Thank you.'

As she dismounted the scooter, a cheerful voice startled the pair.

'Morning, pickle!' Carole had come out of the café to join them. She was a cheerful White woman a few years older than Baz. Her frilly, grandmotherly clothes – you never knew what Carole might wear on any given day – disguised a body honed by hours spent in the gym every day.

The young man looked at Carole. 'Good morning. Mrs Ballard, innit?'

'Ballard sounds like bollard and everyone knows those are just architectural nuisances.'

Baz smiled at her friend. 'Good morning, Carole. How are you?' She deposited her keys into the pocket of her cardigan. They weighed her down in a strange and lopsided way. She hoped they wouldn't rip a hole in the flimsy fabric.

'Peggy sent me out here to make sure you're aware of the chemtrails. It's Napoleon and Tony Blair at it again – of course it is. Always going to war with one another over control of the Hittite race, you see. And if the chemtrails make contact with your skin, the consequences will be dire.'

Carole prattled on like this as the three of them walked the few metres to the café's entrance. As they passed the front window, Baz spied a woman wearing a beautiful chiffon skirt and floral cardigan.

Oh, that's me! That's my reflection. She fingered the gauzy fabric. Inside the café, the customary scents of coffee and sugar and pastries enveloped her in cosy comfort, allowing her lingering panic to ebb.

Baz turned to her new friend. 'I should get you a coffee too. Or whatever you want. To thank you for coming to my rescue.' And then she remembered. 'Oh, drat.'

The young man placed a gentle hand on her arm. 'It's fine, auntie. I just wanted to make sure you were okay.'

'Thank you.' Baz looked at Carole. 'Would you be so kind as to place my order for me? I'm afraid I don't have my wallet.'

Carole chuckled. 'Orders? Good gravy, no! They wouldn't let someone like *me* take orders. Have you not listened to a single one of my stories?' She booped Baz on the nose before turning and heading into the coffee shop's second room. 'Baz wants me to take holy orders! Can you even imagine?' She dropped heavily onto her seat on the small sofa, giggling gleefully.

A full-figured Black woman wearing a very smart yet comfortable-looking red dress looked up. 'Jerome Evans, is that you? How do you know our Ms Spencer?' Madge always seemed to know everyone in the neighbourhood. She was the most social person Baz knew. And heaven knew Madge's people skills had frequently come in handy.

The young man, Jerome, guided Baz into the second room. 'Morning, Mrs Dixon.' He nodded at Peggy. 'Auntie. Your friend was mugged. I walked her the rest of the way here to make sure she was safe.'

Amidst her friends' cries of shock and outrage, Baz settled herself into her usual chair. 'Thank you, Jerome.' She made to pick up her teacup before realising she didn't have one. Cookie, Peggy's enormous Alsatian, crawled out from under the low table and came to sit on Baz's feet, tickling her toes through her sandals. He arched his back and pressed his face into her armpit. She buried her fingers into his fur, letting his calm nature flow into her.

Peggy looked up from her laptop, her fingers still perched on the keys. Her short, spiky hair was freshly dyed – not just its usual hot pink but a whole rainbow of colours. 'I hope you got a good look at the culprits.' Her hair was stunning. Baz thought she looked radiant – despite her seventy-some years.

'I'll send Harvey Junior to deal with the bastards,' added Carole.

Jerome rubbed his hand over his face. He looked as though he were trying to erase himself. 'Sorry. I shoulda tried to get a pic of the number plate.'

'Number plate?' Madge repeated it back as a question. 'What in heaven's name are you talking about, Jerome?' Madge had also changed her hair since Friday. Today, she sported a very sleek and stylish chin-length bob.

'His hands were otherwise occupied.' Several eyebrows

raised at that. 'If not for his lightning reflexes, I would have fallen off my scooter.' Baz thought she was seeing spots – though it could have been her eyes struggling to adapt to the lower levels of light indoors. 'He caught me,' she clarified. Well, tried to clarify. She wasn't sure if it helped.

'The thief was on a moped,' Jerome said.

Baz leant forwards to pick up her tea once more – before remembering there still wasn't any to pick up. Her hands were shaking.

'I see.' Madge lowered her glasses so she could peer directly at the young man. 'Jerome, would you be so kind as to go ask Sarah to bring Ms Spencer her usual order and to place it on my tab? Tell her to make haste. And you can get yourself a coffee as well.' Her hands were still busy with her knitting – a lovely teal jumper.

Jerome nodded, relief washing over his features. 'Of course, auntie.' He escaped back into the other room.

Madge gave a quick nod before turning to Baz. 'Now what's all this about being mugged?'

Clasping a hand to her chest, Baz took a slow, deep breath. 'I'm fine. I'll be fine.'

Madge and Peggy shared one of their looks – born from years of friendship. Carole waved at a pigeon outside on the road.

After a few moments, Peggy made a rolling motion with her hand. Her short fingernails were due for a repaint – most of the black polish had flaked off. 'We know you *will be* fine, Baz. But you're clearly not fine now. What happened?'

Her heart rate was finally drifting back down to its normal pace. 'I was on my way here, when I felt a sudden crash. I was lucky Jerome was there to assist. I didn't even realise what had hit me, but someone on a moped grabbed my handbag. By the time I looked up, they were crossing the lights at the bottom of the high street. Running a red, in fact. They got my phone, my wallet – everything.'

Madge kissed her teeth. 'What's becoming of this neighbourhood? A woman can't go for a stroll in broad daylight.'

Peggy nodded. 'Disgraceful!'

Without letting go of her knitting, Madge reached over and tapped Peggy on the knee. 'It's just like what happened with your laptop.'

Peggy cast her eyes down to Madge's hand and looked up at the woman herself until she withdrew her hand. 'I am very well aware of my missing device. We've spoken about it countless times over the last few months. I'm bored of talking about it.'

Madge's needles returned to their rapid click-clacking. 'You were burgled in the middle of the aftern—'

'We know all this.' Peggy rolled her eyes. 'Everyone here knows what happened. Our flat was burgled three months ago while Carole and I had lunch with her daughter. And I'll grant you it was an interesting topic ... for the first week or so. But I'm seventy-six years old and I don't wish to spend my remaining decades covering the same topic over and over again.'

Baz suspected Peggy was still processing the trauma of having her home – her personal space – invaded. But Peggy was a woman of analysis and action – she wasn't one for talking about her feelings.

Madge frowned at Peggy. 'There's no cause for interrupting me.'

Peggy focused her gaze on the screen of her replacement device. 'And there's no cause for laying hands on me.'

Madge harrumphed. 'Oh, please. I touched your knee. Don't be so dramatic.'

Peggy and Madge's verbal sparring matches used to make Baz uncomfortable. But, these days, the pair's spats only gave her mild butterflies in her tummy – they no longer left her clenching every muscle. She knew it was all bluff and bluster; there was no venom in it. The two women clearly loved one another a great deal.

Platonic love, naturally. Peggy was madly in love with Carole. And Madge was straight. But the love was real all the same.

Sarah, Madge's youngest daughter, bustled through the door. 'Ms Spencer!' She laid a tray on the table in front of the women and placed one hand on Baz's shoulder and another on Cookie's head. 'Jerome just told me what happened. Are you okay?'

While Sarah spoke, Madge bent forwards and poured Baz's tea. She added oat milk from the little pot and a spoonful of sugar, then slid the cup towards her friend. Baz didn't normally take sugar – though somewhere in the back of her mind she knew that was something you did for shock.

'Ta.' Baz reached out and picked up the tea, clutching it to herself and breathing in the vapours. 'I'm fine, Sarah. Thank you. Or, at least, I will be.'

Sarah stood. 'You sure? Have you called the police already or do you need someone to do that for you?'

Having taken a long sip of the life-infusing beverage, Baz lowered her mug to her lap. 'I'll be all right. Thank you. I'll ring them from home this afternoon once I'm feeling more myself.'

Sarah gave Baz's shoulder a quick squeeze before ducking back through to the main room.

Jerome poked his head through the doorway and lifted his coffee in thanks. 'You ladies all right? Only I'm already late to work.'

'Thank you, Jerome.' Baz nodded at the young man who'd come to her rescue.

'We've got it from here,' Peggy added.

Jerome looked at Baz. 'I'm glad I was able to help – even in a small way.' With a wave, he turned and headed out.

'What did these ruffians get?' Madge peered closely at her knitting before resuming.

'My whole bag.' Baz touched the soft fabric of her scarf. 'It had my phone, my wallet, some lipstick, my sunglasses – everything.' She bit down on her lips to keep herself from crying. 'Oh! My embroidery. I hadn't even considered that.'

She took another sip of her tea, trying to think of all the good things in her life. 'I shouldn't be such a ninny. I have my health. I have Daisy and wonderful friends.' She waved a hand at the women around her. 'I have my flat. I've been able to retire relatively young. My life is good. I shouldn't—' She pressed her knuckles to her lips and focused on her breathing.

'Your life *is* good.' Madge peered over her glasses at Baz. 'That doesn't mean you're not allowed to be affected by this.'

Peggy nodded. 'You've had a traumatic experience. Give yourself five minutes to recover, eh?'

Carole, who had seemed to be a million miles away, got up and sidled over to Baz. 'I haven't got my knitting with me today, but if you need me to pop home and get my needles, just say the word.' She patted Baz's arm.

Baz fought the tears that were threatening to fall. 'Sorry, I don't know how to knit.'

Carole laughed uproariously. 'You silly mongoose. I meant my *special* needles. You know, for dealing with—'

Baz cut her strange friend off before she said anything incriminating, thanking her with a smile. She was touched by Carole's kind, if slightly murderous, offer.

Carole patted her arm once more then returned to her seat.

Unable to put words to what she was feeling, Baz focused on drinking her tea. It hadn't really been strong enough when Madge poured it – but that was beside the point. It was tea. It possessed almost magical restorative powers. She finished the contents of the cup, then leant forwards and poured another from the lovely floral teapot. Once she'd added a splash of oat milk, she picked up the cup and leant back in her chair.

After a few minutes, she felt like she was almost back to herself. With a quiet sigh, she set the cup down and then bent to pick up her— 'Oh, drat! My embroidery. I was nearly finished with that piece. You know, the one with the picture of Cookie?' She wrapped her arms around the dog in question, hugging him close.

in which we all just want to be loved and accepted

HALF AN HOUR LATER, Baz was beginning to feel better about things when the bell above the door clanged. She leant forwards in her chair to see if anyone she knew was arriving. Somehow, no matter how much time she spent at Wellbeloved, she just couldn't get past the habit. All the more so when she had nothing to occupy herself.

In this case, though, the short man with light brown skin who entered was entirely familiar. Her heart warmed when she saw him. *Paul!* His short hair was neat as a pin and his bold eyeglasses and customary bow tie combined to give him a dapper air.

Paul gave her a little wave as he went to queue for his coffee. Baz suspected he couldn't afford to splurge very often – but she'd got him a gift card for his birthday last month. He'd been treating himself to a cup once a week ever since.

Despite herself, she wondered, *What am I thinking – starting a new relationship at my age? Sixty-three is no kind of age to be dating!*

'—no idea what's caused it,' said Peggy.

Baz shook her head to clear it. 'Sorry, Peggy. I was miles away. What was that?'

With an eyebrow arched, Peggy winked at her.

Madge looked up from her knitting, her new bobbed hairstyle artfully framing her face. 'Wasn't that your beau who just came in?' Baz was certain Madge knew it was – the woman never missed a thing.

Baz cleared her throat as daintily as she could. 'Yes, that was Paul.'

Carole pulled her embroidery from her bag – Baz had taught her how to embroider a few months ago.

Laying her hoop out on her lap, Carole said, 'They say it was Saul of Tarsus who became Paul the Apostle. But, of course, there's absolutely no credible evidence for that at all. What can you expect, though? Hardly anything remains of the ancient teachings.' She was working on a piece depicting the beheading of Charles the First. A gratuitously graphic piece in Baz's opinion – not that she'd say so to Carole, of course.

'Anyhow,' said Peggy, drawing the word out. 'As I was saying, Baz, I spoke with Tina last night. Something's wrong. I couldn't get her to tell me what it is. But she's not herself.'

Tina was Carole's youngest, Baz knew that much. She'd met her once. Tina had several foster children. A few months back, she'd visited the school across from the café about one of the girls in her care. After the meeting, she'd stopped in to have a coffee with her mum and the rest of the gang.

Baz was about to ask Peggy in what way Tina wasn't herself, but just then Paul walked into the café's second room with another man. 'Sweet pea.' He bent and kissed Baz on the cheek before turning to the other women. 'Morning, ladies.'

The other man nodded at the women. 'Good morning.' He was tall – probably about six feet. He was Black, about their age, and dressed quite formally. And familiar, though without context, Baz was struggling to place him.

Paul gestured at the other man. 'This is Jimi. We met while we were waiting to place our orders just now. He's new around here, having just moved from north London. I said I'd introduce him to a few people.' He looked at Jimi. 'Naturally, I'm starting with these lovely ladies. Jimi, this is Baz. That's Madge. And those two over there are Peggy and her partner Carole.'

Everyone exchanged pleasantries for a few moments until Carole interjected. 'You've come to escape the nuclear testing of course. Tottenham rhymes with rotten ham and we all know what that implies. You're lucky they let you leave.'

Jimi blinked. 'I *am* from Tottenham, as it happens. How did you know?'

Madge set her knitting on her lap and bent down to pour herself another cup of tea. The ruby red liquid flowed from her own special thermal carafe. A cloud of steam enveloped her, fogging up her glasses. 'What brought you to Deptford, Jimi?' She leant back in her chair and looked up at him.

'I always dreamt of opening my own business, see. Wanted to work for myself. Be my own man, right?' All eyes focused on him as he spoke. 'I saved for all my life and I've finally done it. Opened a little shop last month. I'd like to invite you fine ladies to come and check it out.'

Baz clapped. 'Olujimi Adewale! I knew you looked familiar – but I was struggling to place you. You're the new tenant in the unit on Deptford Broadway.' She looked at her friends. 'That new bookshop next to the daycare.'

Earlier that year, the landlord had tried to double the rent on the daycare centre. Sarah had asked her mother to help out, figuring she could talk some sense into the man. She probably hadn't expected Madge and her friends to blackmail the man into selling Baz the whole building at a bargain-basement price.

Jimi lifted his hands. 'Ah, and you're my landlady. Mrs Spencer, right?'

Baz grinned. 'It's *Ms* Spencer, actually. But please call me Baz.'

Reaching into his pockets, Jimi pulled out a series of leaflets advertising the bookshop. Something escaped his grip and tumbled across the floor, landing next to Baz's chair. She bent down to pick it up. A small spray bottle with prescription details on the side. Nitrolingual.

He handed each of the women one of the flyers. 'Please, you must come to the shop. I'll put on an excellent welcome for you. And those flyers give you a discount on your first purchase.'

He handed papers to each of them. When he got to Baz, she swapped the paper for the medicine. 'I think you dropped this.'

'Thank you.' His eyes opened wide. 'Mustn't lose my meds.' He tapped his heart before dropping the bottle back into his pocket.

The papers were pink and covered in hearts. Madge squinted at hers through her specs. 'Broadway Books – your local source for love.'

Jimi motioned at the leaflet in her hand. 'We specialise in romance novels – and other books about love.'

'Jimi, did I tell you I work at the local library?' Paul stood to Baz's side, running his fingers along the edge of the paper. 'Books are something of a passion for me – and romance books? Yes, please! Who doesn't love a good romance? After all, everyone wants to be loved – am I right?' After stuffing the paper in his pocket, he adjusted his bow tie.

'Romance books? Ooh, I do love a bit of smut!' Madge looked up at Jimi, peering over the top of her glasses. 'And Peggy here writes very popular romance novels. Not enough *heat* for my tastes – but I'm sure they're very good if you like that sort of thing. Maybe you could stock them in your shop?'

Jimi nodded as he turned to look at Peggy. 'Is that so? What sort of romance novels?'

'The kind where men shamelessly love other men.' Coming from Peggy, the words almost sounded like a dare.

Jimi's eyes lit up – and Baz knew immediately that Peggy had judged him wrong. 'Excellent! I'm sure we can come to some sort of arrangement. And maybe you can recommend some other authors in your genre – that will help round out my shelves nicely!'

If Baz hadn't been watching her friend, she'd have missed Peggy's blink. 'I'd be happy to help.'

'And now, I should get back.' Jimi stabbed a thumb in the direction of the exit. 'Mustn't keep my customers waiting all day. It was lovely meeting such beautiful ladies.' He seemed to focus most of his attention on Madge with this last bit. He bowed his head at Paul. 'And gentleman. I hope I'll see you all at my shop before long.'

He ducked through the door to the main room, then stopped and turned back. 'And I meant it, Peggy. I want to read your books. Please come by.'

As soon as the main door clicked shut behind Jimi, Paul bent and planted a gentle kiss on Baz's cheek. 'I only stopped in for a quick hello. Time for me to head out. I didn't mean to intrude on your girls' morning – I've got to get to the library in time for my shift.'

He studied her for a moment. 'Are you okay, sweet pea? You're not yourself this morning.'

Paul really was a wonderful man – why was she holding back in her relationship with him? Why couldn't she stop herself from overthinking everything? 'Something happened this morning. But I'm fine – I promise. I'll tell you about it later. But everything will be fine.'

He took both of her hands in his. 'You're sure?'

'I am. I'll be fine.' And even as she said it, she realised it was true. No one had been hurt – that was all that mattered. She'd been mildly inconvenienced. Her cards could be replaced easily enough. She'd need to get a new phone but she wasn't short of funds. The embroidery work would need to be redone but, well, essentially ... so what?

'All right. If you're sure. I'll speak to you later, then.' He straightened his bow tie before turning to the other women and bidding them farewell.

As Baz turned back to face her friends, Madge indicated the front window. 'Would you look at that.'

The women had met Mitch, also known as Crispin Caspian Todd-Mitchell, six months before. His right foot was encased in one of those walking boots they give you when you've broken your ankle. Catching them looking at him, he smiled genially – even doffing an imaginary cap – before carrying on his way.

'Well.' Peggy made a noise something like a strangled laugh. 'That's for the books.'

'Mmm hmm.' Madge concurred. 'I'd never thought we'd see a smile out of that man.' She shook her head. 'Now, where were we?'

Without her embroidery, Baz wasn't sure what to do with her hands. 'Peggy, you were talking about Tina. You thought something was wrong.' Baz waggled and flexed her fingers.

Carole rummaged around in her craft bag. She pulled out several embroidery hoops, before selecting one and tossing it to Baz without a word. It nearly pinged her in the eye, but she managed to bat it away. Next, Carole slid her case of needles, threads, and other bits across the sofa towards Baz, who was grateful she hadn't thrown them.

Baz bent and picked up the hoop. 'Thank you, Carole. That's very kind.' It contained a striking image of an eagle paired with words. She supposed she could adjust it on the fly to replace the profanity with 'flip' – though that put her in mind of Peggy's sister. Oh, and she'd have to replace a few other words as well. She just wasn't as crass as Carole – not that there was anything wrong with that. May as well get started with the bird. She'd figure out what to do about the words later.

While Baz set about choosing a needle and thread, Peggy responded to her question. 'Tina and the kids were meant to come to ours for dinner last night but she cancelled at the last minute. She said it was because she's on deadline—'

Madge kissed her teeth. 'Sounds like she's being responsible.'

Peggy glowered at her friend. '—but I happen to know she's still got almost four weeks.' She paused before continuing. 'Ordinarily, when Tina and I get chatting, we'll have a good old natter. We can talk for hours, especially when it comes to our craft.'

Baz must've had a puzzled look on her face because Peggy clarified. 'Tina's an author. She also edits my books – but that's as may be.'

'Oh! Aren't you a pair of peas in a pod.' Baz's eyebrows lifted. 'What sort of thing does she write – anything I might've read?'

Peggy winked. 'Almost certainly.'

As she pushed the needle through the taut fabric, Baz stabbed herself in the finger. Grimacing, she pulled her injured finger into her mouth. Luckily, she hadn't drawn blood this time. She'd started using thimbles a few months ago after making herself bleed one too many times. But her kit was on the back of some kid's moped. And Carole was far too dextrous for thimbles.

Realising she'd been silent for too long, Baz looked up. 'I'm not sure I follow. What does she write?'

Madge grunted. 'Celebrity nonsense.'

'She's a ghostwriter.' Peggy cast her friend another dirty look. 'You know when some big so-and-so publishes a novel or their autobiography?'

Baz nodded.

'In most cases, the star hasn't actually written it,' Peggy said. 'The publisher hires a ghostwriter, who interviews them about their ideas. Then they write the book, and the actor, musician, politician, or what have you takes all the credit.'

Madge rubbed her fingers together. 'And pockets all the cash.'

Peggy cocked her head. 'Touché. Though to be fair, the ghostwriter usually gets a fairly hefty chunk of change as well.'

'And this is what Tina does?' Baz turned the embroidery hoop over and tied off the thread.

'I doubt she's worked with any of the *really* big names,' Peggy replied. 'But big enough that she's doing all right financially. Obviously, she's sworn to strict secrecy – can't tell us who she's writing for. But I've got my guesses.'

Baz snipped off a length of grey embroidery thread before threading it into the needle. 'And you think she was making excuses for last night?'

'She probably had a hot date.' Madge poured more of her red tea.

Baz cringed as her friend drank the steaming liquid – she preferred to let her tea cool down a bit before drinking it. Imagine wilfully scalding your mouth like that!

'I wouldn't blame the girl for wanting a bit of action.' Peggy shook her head. 'But I don't think it was that. Something's wrong. I just wish I knew what it was.'

Madge frowned. 'You know what kids are like these days. She'll tell you when she's ready.'

Looking directly at Madge, Peggy replied, 'Kids? Tina's thirty-six years old, Madge.'

Resting her embroidery on her lap, Baz leant forwards and poured herself another cup of tea, knowing that this exchange could go on for quite some time.

'I know what age she is. She shares a birthday with my youngest.'

'Your youngest.' Peggy rolled her eyes. 'Madge, Sarah owns her own business. She's been running this coffee shop for three years. She's married with two ch—'

'Two perfectly lovely children – my youngest grandbabies,' Madge continued. 'Doesn't change the fact that—'

'Where were you at in your life when you were thirty-six?' Peggy wagged a finger at Madge.

Baz breathed in the scent of her tea and let it infuse her with a sense of peace.

Madge leant back in her chair. 'Well now, let's see. When I was thirty-six, Stanley and I had been married for four years. Sarah was a toddler. Winston and Cheryl were at primary school. Em and Tony were at secondary school. Julie had just left for university and I was thinking of joining her. I'd been an RN for more than a decade and I was ready to go back and become a nurse prac—'

Peggy tossed both hands in the air. 'So you weren't a child!'

'Well, of course, *I* wasn't a child.' Madge looked indignant. 'I was a grown adult wi—'

'You don't see the hypocrisy in your own statement, do you?'

The two of them bickered good-naturedly until it was time for the women to head to their respective homes.

Madge had offered to accompany Baz to the police station, but Baz assured her she'd be fine on her own. First things first, she wanted to get home and eat some lunch. Fortunately, the thief hadn't got her keys; the key ring included the one that was plugged into the scooter at the time.

———

BY THE TIME she opened the door to her flat, Baz had come up with a plan for the afternoon. First up, call and cancel her cards. Then, she'd check her iPad to see if she'd missed any calls or texts. After that, she'd heat up some leftovers for lunch. Once she was ready, she'd contact the police.

Baz parked the scooter in the hall and took off her shoes. It struck her that, without a landline, she'd need the iPad in order to call the bank. She mentally adjusted the order of her to-do list.

In her bedroom, she dug the old device out from the dresser. The battery was dead, so she brought it through to the office off the living room and plugged it in. It would need a few minutes before she'd be able to turn it on.

In the fridge, she found a single serving of the vegan Thai soup Daisy had made for last night's dinner. The girl was such a good cook – she was so lucky to have her. 'We're lucky to have one another,' Baz reminded herself. She popped the container into the microwave and returned to her desk.

Baz picked up the iPad. An unexpected name appeared on the home screen. When she clicked on it, the words made her drop the device to the floor, cracking its screen.

After letting out a few words she'd never admit to using, she fumbled to pick it back up – and very nearly dropped it all over again.

HARI

I miss you. Call me?

wherein a smart decision costs someone

PEGGY PACKED HER LAPTOP – her *new* laptop – into its carry bag and stood up. She put on her sunglasses, picked up Cookie's lead, and accepted Carole's hand. The four women bade farewell before heading in separate directions.

Peggy kissed Carole on the cheek and handed her Cookie's lead as well as her laptop bag. 'Just need to pick up the noodles for lunch.'

'My mother's sons were angry with me,' said Carole. 'They made me the keeper of the vineyards. But my own vineyard I have not kept.'

'And a bottle of wine, okay. I'll see you in ten.' Peggy enjoyed the warmth of the summer sun as she joined the throngs of pedestrians waiting to cross the main road.

Despite what Peggy had said at the café, she was still upset about the break-in.

As the light changed to walk, Peggy thought about that Saturday afternoon, three months ago, when they'd dropped Cookie off with Baz for the afternoon while they had gone to spend some time with Tina.

Peggy would have loved to take Cookie with her – but poor Cookie was petrified by Tina's dog. At three kilograms, Montrese the Maltese was about the size of one of Cookie's paws – but she was a holy menace. She absolutely adored people, including children, but she would terrorise any dog that came within spitting distance of her.

That day's experience still weighed on Peggy as the shop's automated doors slid open.

It had been a cool grey day in April. They'd had a lovely afternoon with Tina. But when they got home, they found their flat door had been jimmied. Peggy's heart had been in her throat when she'd pushed the door aside and entered. The place had been turned over. Cupboards had been ransacked, drawers had had their contents dumped on the floor, and furniture had been tossed around. But the laptop was the only thing Peggy could confirm was missing. Maybe some papers – she wasn't entirely certain.

Taking the noodles and the wine to the cash register, Peggy had a brief chat with the cashier as she paid for her purchases. Once she was finished, she stepped back out into the summer sun.

When they'd discovered the burglary, Peggy had wanted to call the police. But Carole wasn't having it. It wasn't surprising. The Ballard family and the police didn't exactly see eye to eye. So, in the end, Carole had told Harvey Junior, who promised to look into the matter. And Peggy had had a quiet chat with Madge's grandson Peter, who was a constable with the Met police. He knew Carole and understood her reticence to bring the law in – and Peggy trusted him.

When the light changed, Peggy crossed back to the south side of New Cross Road and made her way towards home.

Peter had urged her to report the burglary. But, when pressed, he'd admitted there wasn't a lot the police could or would do about it. He'd told her it would be important to get a police reference number before making a claim against their home insurance. Peggy had actually guffawed at that. Imagine making a claim for a laptop worth a measly four hundred quid. Their insurance premiums would skyrocket – forever.

Peggy unlocked the front door of her building, taking care that no one followed her in. To her chagrin, she'd found herself becoming more cautious since the incident. When she got to her door, she looked around before putting her key in the lock.

The landlord had replaced the door more quickly than Peggy would have expected. She suspected Harvey Junior had something to do with that. Carole's eldest son could be … persuasive.

'I'm back.' Peggy carried her shopping bag through to the kitchen to start prepping lunch. Cookie wagged his tail and followed her.

She found Carole sharpening their knives – something she did far more regularly than even the most dedicated chefs probably did. 'Here you go, my love.' She tossed a paring knife into the air. Peggy would have flinched if she hadn't been confident in Carole's abilities. Having caught the deadly blade by the handle, Carole spun it around and passed it to Peggy.

'Cheers.' Peggy set to work, dicing an onion and then a cabbage, tossing the strips into a hot pan as she went. 'Boil that kettle for me and put the noodles to soak, would you, my love?'

As she filled the kettle, Carole waved her favourite rolling pin around, like an American cheerleader with a baton.

After the burglary, Peggy's nephew, Alex, had offered to buy her a replacement laptop. But she hadn't accepted a penny of her family's money in more than fifty years. Oh, sure. She let him send her a subscription of coffee beans from his little side business – but that was quid pro quo. It was a thank you for setting him up with the contract to supply

Wellbeloved. But no way was she letting him buy her a new computer.

With the cabbage and onion mix caramelising nicely, Peggy set to work on a block of tofu.

Harvey Junior had offered to replace her computer too – through Carole, naturally. Peggy had never felt welcomed by the Ballard family. With the exception of Tina and her foster kids, that is. And if Peggy wasn't going to take money from her own family for a new laptop, she wasn't going to accept one from Harvey Junior. It would almost certainly be one that had fallen off the back of a lorry, as the saying goes.

Peggy gave the mix in the wok a stir and then began slicing a carrot. She considered the two competing offers – both of which she'd declined. She'd had no doubt that each came with its own strings, though neither would have been revealed until after the fact, naturally.

Instead, she'd used her own meagre savings to buy a three-year-old refurbished laptop, thank you very much. Truth be told, it was a step up from her previous one. She quite enjoyed the larger screen. Not that her eyes weren't perfectly good. She definitely did *not* need glasses.

It was taking time to replace all her favourite stickers, though. She'd managed to procure one that said 'still hate Thatcher', an anti-Brexit one, a rainbow one, and a few rock band ones. But there had been one she'd really liked; it featured a clown on a unicycle and the words 'mock the patriarchy'. She'd yet to find a replacement.

Peggy drained the noodles and added them to the wok, before smothering the whole mix in satay sauce. Tossing the concoction around in the pan for a bit with one hand, she used the other to add a healthy fistful of beansprouts. She plated it all up and joined Carole at the dining table.

Once the lunch dishes were washed, dried, and put away,

Carole headed out for her afternoon session at the local gym. As soon as the door closed behind her, Peggy sat down at the dining table and opened the screen of her laptop. Then she pulled out her mobile and fired off a quick text.

PEGGY

Urgent. Zoom, now.

She felt a small pang of guilt for manipulating the girl like this. It was a calculated move – one she'd been planning since Tina had cancelled their dinner plans the night before.

The response came through as quickly as she expected.

TINA

omw

Peggy shared a link, then launched the call. Her own face filled the screen and Peggy experienced a brief start at the sight of her rainbow hair. She sat tall and breathed deep as she ran a hand over the sides. Her image shrank as a second box was added to the window – black background with white text reading, 'C.J. Ballard (she/her)'.

It took a few seconds, but the black box flickered and was replaced by a young woman with peachy skin and chin-length brown hair against an orange background. 'Peggy. What is it? Did something happen to Mum? Are you okay?' The tendons on her neck stood out in stark relief and she was chewing on a fingernail.

Peggy held her hands up. 'Your mother is fine. There's noth—'

Tina's knuckles were white as she pressed a fist to her lips. 'Cook—'

'Cookie's fine. We're all fine – I promise. I apologise for scaring you with my text – but I was worried you'd reject anything other than urgency.' Peggy made her voice as soothing as she could. 'It's you I'm worried about. Hence the reason for this call.'

Tina forced air out noisily through her nose. 'I told you – I'm fine, Peggy.'

Peggy leant back in her chair and fixed her stepdaughter with a stare. 'You're not fine. Your hair is lank and there are pronounced shadows beneath your eyes.' She squinted at the screen. 'And if I'm not mistaken, there's food on your collar.'

Tina looked down, first at one side and then the other. She lifted the edge of her shirt to her nose. 'Peanut butter! How the hell...' She shook her head. 'Outward appearances don't mean anything.'

Peggy inclined her head. 'They don't. Lord knows I'm not pressing you to conform to societal beauty norms – but I do believe in taking pride in oneself. Appearances can communicate information about where we're at mentally. The fact you haven't fixed your hair doesn't matter to me. But I suspect you haven't washed it recently – and I know that matters to *you*. The bags under your eyes tell me you're either dehydrated or exhausted. I'm worried about—'

'Peggy, stop!'

'Tina.' They sat that way for a minute. Peggy was starting to think this call had been in vain. 'You matter to me. I want you to be happy. Not all the time – that's not feasible. But on the whole. The way you cancelled on your mother and me last night tells me something isn't right. I'm asking you to tell me what's wrong. I promise – we'll figure it out together.'

'It's...' Tina heaved a sigh. 'Fine. It's this guy. And, no, I do not want you to set Mum or Harvey Junior on him.'

Peggy chuckled at the thought of that. 'Okay. Fair enough. Your mother isn't home right now. Your brother won't go after him.' *I might, though*, she definitely didn't say aloud. 'Just tell me what happened.'

Tina visibly deflated. 'It started so well. He was really, really nice. And he was ... into me, you know? It's been a long time since anyone's paid me any attention like that.'

Peggy pursed her lips. 'I'm sorry, love. You deserve the very best in a life partner.'

Tina had had bad luck with relationships. It wasn't that she wasn't desirable – the problem was she lacked confidence in herself.

'Whatever.' Tina waved Peggy's words away – as she always did whenever the topic turned to love. 'It obviously wasn't real anyway.'

'Wasn't real?' Peggy repeated. 'What do you mean it wasn't real?'

Tina was chewing on her bottom lip so hard Peggy worried she'd draw blood.

'Tina, tell me what happened.'

Shaking her head, Tina whispered, 'I think it was all a scam. A money thing, I mean.'

Peggy bit her tongue to keep from saying anything. She waited for Tina to continue.

'For the first few weeks everything was great. Steve was so attentive and kind and funny. But then after a few weeks, he needed to borrow money. Just a hundred quid and only for two days. He was so sorry about it.'

She covered her face with her hands before continuing. 'And the thing is, I said to myself then that this was a scam. I knew it. I *knew* it! But I was hooked. And so I told myself that I could spare the money – it was worth it to see if he was real. So I paid it but I decided that if he didn't pay it back when he said he would... If there was any delay at all – *any*, even an hour – then I would know it was a scam and I'd get out.'

Peggy nodded. 'That's my clever girl.'

Tina dropped her hands and snorted. 'Only I wasn't so clever – was I?'

'He didn't pay it back,' Peggy said.

Tina laughed, tears streaming down her face. 'What – the hundred quid? Sure he did. Right on time. So, I thought, "See, he is who he says he is. Steve's a good man after all."' She snorted again. 'What an idiot I am.'

She wasn't an idiot – far from it. She was a competent, capable, highly intelligent woman. She had a tendency to trust too easily, though. It was something both Peggy and Carole had tried to encourage her away from, but without much success. Peggy was incredibly heartened to hear Tina'd had the presence of mind to test this unknown lout as far as she did.

But clearly there was more to the story than she'd heard so far. So Peggy held her tongue and waited for Tina to continue.

'The next time he asked for money, it was a bit more – £250. And he needed it for longer. But I was so invested, you know? We'd been talking daily by this point. I really felt like we had a connection. It's been ... a long time since I've had that kind of relationship, innit?' Montrese leapt up onto Tina's lap and snuggled into her. 'Oh, hello, you.'

Peggy nodded but said nothing.

'And then a bit more and a bit more. But it all came to a head on Saturday night. It's Bella, right? She's in kennels while he's away. And she had an accident – she accidentally ate—' She slapped her forehead, startling Montrese. 'Oh my days! She doesn't even exist – does she? I'm such a—'

'Stop.' Peggy held up a finger. 'Let's go through this one thing at a time.'

Tina sniffed and wiped her nose on her sleeve. 'Okay.'

'Bella's a dog, I take it? Or a cat?' Peggy asked.

'Dog,' Tina said without looking up.

Peggy nodded. 'And what do you mean, "while he's away"?'

Tina bit her lip. 'He's working in Dubai for six months. It's his job, see? He works in finance and they've shipped him over there to set up a new office.'

Peggy blinked at that. 'He started a relationship right before leaving the country for half a year?'

'No, he's halfway through the contract.'

Now Peggy was even more confused. 'What do you mean he's halfway through? How did you meet him?'

Tina still refused to look at Peggy. 'I met him online.'

The pieces began to click into place for Peggy. 'So you've not actually met him.'

Tina returned her focus to the camera, indignant. 'Of course I've met him! What do you take me for?' She followed that with something unintelligible, her words muffled by the dog as she pressed her face to Montrese.

'I beg your pardon, love. You're mumbling. What was that last bit?'

'I mean, I talked to him on the phone.' Tina twisted the ends of her hair and began chewing on it.

Peggy's eyebrows drew together. 'You met him and also you spoke on the phone? Or, when you said you'd met him, what you meant was you'd spoken on the phone? Which is it?' She tried to keep the criticism out of her voice – she knew this wasn't Tina's fault.

Tina crossed her arms over her chest and scowled. 'I didn't come here to be judged.' She leant towards the keyboard, supporting the tiny dog with one hand, clearly intending to disconnect the call.

Peggy raised her hands in surrender. 'I'm sorry, love. No judgement, I swear. I'm only trying to understand.' She cursed herself for being the wrong person to have such a delicate conversation. Even though she felt sympathy for the girl and knew this wasn't her fault, she couldn't keep from sounding condescending. Critical. 'Honestly. I just want to understand. You know I could never think badly of you.'

Tina exhaled slowly. 'No, you're probably right anyway – whatever you're thinking. We spoke on the phone almost daily. But, no, we never met in person.'

Peggy nodded, her mind working a mile a minute. 'Now what was this about the dog?'

'Bella. She's a black lab. If she even exists. Which she probably doesn't.'

Tina was crying again, so Peggy waited. She wished she could make the girl a cup of tea – she wasn't any good with crying people.

After a moment, Tina continued. 'Last week he called to tell me that Bella had swallowed a toy. She needed emergency surgery to remove it or she was going to die. But his credit card wasn't working while he was overseas. He asked me to pay the clinic.'

She sniffed and wiped her nose – with a tissue this time. 'It was almost five thousand pounds. He gave me the bank details and begged me to make the transfer straight away.'

Peggy's heart sank. Five thousand! Tina did all right for herself – but not to the degree that she could spare that kind of money.

Tina sobbed, her voice hitching on every word. 'I ... called ... the clinic.'

'You what?' Peggy felt suddenly lighter.

'I called the clinic. It was the middle of the night, so I knew the only one that would be open was the one over in Camberwell. I've got them saved into my phone, just in case.' Her cheeks burnt bright red. The rest of the words came tumbling out, rapid-fire through curtains of tears. 'Told them I was calling in regard to Bella – that I wanted to double-check the payment details. Said I didn't want her to have to wait for surgery. I knew she was in pain and I wanted her to be operated on straight away. But I just needed to be sure I had the right bank details.'

Peggy bit back a smile. Clever girl! 'What did they say?' Though she was pretty sure she knew the answer.

'They'd never heard of her. Or Steve. And they didn't accept payment by bank transfer.'

in which baz stabs herself — again

Baz felt lighter than air as she drove her scooter towards the café the following morning. Her confidence took a bit of a hit when she passed the spot where she'd been mugged. She reminded herself to be more vigilant ... but her mind kept wandering.

But overall, she was feeling good. Confident. Exhausted – but in a good way. She'd been up most of the night on Face-Time with Hari.

They'd talked and laughed. When she'd asked why he'd called, he'd told her he'd missed her – missed having someone there at the end of each day to talk things through with.

And so she'd told him about her friends – though not about what they sometimes got up to – and her life in London, that she'd taken up embroidery, about the drag shows she'd been to.

For his part, Hari caught her up on all the gossip in her old neighbourhood. Sophie – their German shepherd – had a new girlfriend. Apparently, the people in the house to the left had got a Lhasa Apso puppy and the two dogs were absolutely besotted with one another. And a new family had moved into the house to the right. The husband kept trying to convert Hari to various right-wing conspiracy theories.

Baz had absolutely cackled when Hari had relayed a bit about the man attempting to lecture him on the Canadian criminal justice system. Hari was a barrister with thirty-five years' experience specialising in criminal law. As a KC, he worked mainly in defence cases, but also occasionally worked for the Crown. The idea that a retired social studies teacher should presume to tell him how the justice system worked had Baz howling with laughter.

It felt so good talking to Hari again. Right. Like coming home. She didn't know where the conversation would lead, but she was pleased that they'd opened up the lines of communication again. Elated, almost.

She pulled her scooter into its normal parking place alongside the café and switched off the engine. As she dismounted, Peggy, Carole, and Cookie came into view. Shielding her eyes from the sun with her left hand, she waved. 'Morning, ladies.'

Peggy nodded and Cookie bounded up to Baz for scritches. He was so much like Sophie it hurt. Bigger than her, but so very similar in appearance.

'Oh, Baz, I've been meaning to tell you.' Carole took Baz by the elbow. 'You know about the experiments, right? The ones designed to cause congenital infertility. It's all about replacing the modern Homo sapiens with Etruscans. You go into the dentist for a simple laparoscopic surgery – and next thing you know, you're in a secret underground lab, being pumped to the eyeballs full of anti-growth hormones.'

Peggy pushed the door open and held it for the others to walk through.

Five minutes later, Baz settled into her seat.

Peggy bent down and hefted her laptop into her lap. 'Well.' Removing it from its pouch, she looked across at Baz. 'Are you going to tell us what's got you so smiley today? Can we assume it relates to your little beau?'

With a sharp intake of breath, Baz realised she hadn't once considered Paul since she said goodbye to him yesterday morning when he'd left the café. A vice closed around her chest.

'Oh!' Peggy's eyebrows jumped up towards her hairline. She turned to Carole and gave a little smirk – though Carole's attention appeared to be miles away.

Madge paused her knitting and looked over. 'So, not Paul, then.' She may have been wearing a wig the day before as her hair was now in neat plaits that coiled round her head. The beautiful style must have taken hours to create.

'You've met someone new, then?' Peggy studiously avoided looking at her as she opened her laptop.

'What? No! Of course not!' Baz wasn't sure why her voice cracked like that.

Peggy and Madge exchanged one of those glances that Baz always hated. Well, not hated. Normally, she found those little shared glances endearing. But today it felt like something was stabbing her in the gut.

'Who is he, then?' Madge looked at her, making Baz squirm in her seat.

'Or she,' Peggy added pointedly.

Baz's face warmed – though whether it was driven by shame or elation, she couldn't say – as she pushed the needle through the fabric in her embroidery hoop. 'No, no – it's not – it's – I didn't— Ow!' She stabbed her finger into her mouth and sucked the little pinprick of blood. She really needed to replace her thimble or her fingers were going to suffer.

'So, what *is* it like?' To give Peggy credit, she didn't look like she was hoping for a salacious titbit – more like she was concerned. Her tone was as gentle as Baz had ever heard it.

'We're only teasing, Baz,' Madge said. 'You know we're here for you, right?'

Peggy nodded. 'You won't get any judgement from us.'

Baz was grateful for their kindness. She bit her lip before making her confession. 'I spent several hours last night talking to Hari.'

The look that passed between Madge and Peggy this time felt less suggestive.

'This is Hari the ex-husband, Hari?' Madge asked, eyebrows raised.

Peggy sneered. 'The one who couldn't continue to be with you because of your transition?'

'It's not like that,' Baz said – her voice little more than a low whine. 'You know what? I don't think I'm ready to talk about this. And stop with the looks, you two. I don't need your judgement right now. Can we talk about something else, please?'

'No judgement here.' Peggy raised her hands in surrender. 'On my honour. We don't have to talk about it if you don't want.'

'But you know we're always here for you, right?' Madge leant across the space between them and touched her knee.

'Thank you.' Baz was beyond grateful for her friends. 'But let's talk about something else now, please.' Tears welled in her eyes. Due to the pain in her finger, of course.

There was a pause then, during which Peggy watched her – presumably waiting to see whether Baz was going to say anything more on the subject of her ex-husband.

She wasn't.

'All right then,' Peggy began, drawing the word out while keeping her eyes fixed on Baz. 'I spoke to Tina yesterday. Had a good long chat with her.'

Madge paused her knitting and peered over her glasses at Peggy.

Baz, grateful the attention was no longer focused on her, took the opportunity to pour a cup of tea. 'How's she doing? Did you get to the bottom of what's been bothering her?' She breathed in the calming, soothing aromas before taking a drink. *Is there anything better in all the world than a good cup of tea?*

Peggy whistled softly. 'Hoo, did I ever. You're not going to believe this—'

'Well, we certainly won't if you don't tell us.'

'That was a very *me* thing to say, Madge,' replied Peggy. 'Is my personality finally rubbing off on you?'

In response, Madge simply scowled.

'I managed to get Tina on video yesterday.' Peggy proceeded to tell the women about how Tina had been conned.

'That's terrible.' Baz knotted the thread she'd been using and snipped off the excess. She selected a pretty pink from Carole's supplies and began work on the lettering. Instead of changing the offensive words, she'd swapped out some vowels for asterisks.

'If Diane and Harvey Junior get their hands on the villain behind this scam, he won't be anything more than a stain on the pavement.' Carole's voice was as cheery as ever.

Peggy pointed a finger in her partner's direction. 'I promised her they wouldn't. Mind you, I didn't promise her *we* wouldn't. I managed to get a few details out of her. I very much doubt they're true, but they can help us build up a picture. He's originally from New York but he's lived in London for six years. He's forty-nine years old. Full name is Stephen Wright.'

Baz tittered. 'Mr Right?'

Peggy cocked her head. 'Just so.'

Madge's nostrils flared. 'That poor girl.'

'Thankfully, she had the good sense to call the vet clinic to verify things.' Peggy picked a bit of fluff off her jeans. 'Even still, all told, the bastard managed to fleece her for almost four grand.'

Madge made a noise like she was choking. 'Four thousand pounds?'

'It's not her fault,' Peggy said through clenched teeth.

Baz's arms felt stiff. 'These fraudsters are becoming increasingly slick. Their operations are—'

'Yes, I know that,' Madge snapped. She seemed to reconsider before raising a hand in surrender. 'I'm sorry. That was rude of me.'

'Madge, are you okay?' It occurred to Baz that her friend had been uncharacteristically short and snippy over the past few days. She wished she'd noticed sooner.

'I'm sorry. I shouldn't have been so curt with you ladies.' Madge's knitting needles were rapidly click-clacking away. 'I think I've been feeling listless since Bibi and Gul left the flat. I don't like living on my own – it always leaves me grumpier than I like to be. But I shouldn't take it out on you, ladies.'

Madge volunteered with an organisation that matched her with asylum seekers. She'd been hosting a string of people in her home for well over a decade – refugees from various countries. A couple from Pakistan, a gay man from Uganda, a Ukrainian mother and child. Madge had thrown a party for the most recent pair when they moved into their own accommodation just last month. It had been a lovely evening.

'Have you got new people moving in?' Baz felt for her friend. She didn't think she'd want to live alone either. And the programme really was a lifeline for people abandoned by society.

'No, I spoke to the young woman who runs the charity just the other day. They don't have anyone suitable right now. It won't be long, though – it never is.' Madge looked over at

Peggy. 'So, back to Tina... This rogue fleeced her for thousands of pounds, you say?' She kissed her teeth. 'Disgraceful.'

Baz poured a second cup of tea. 'It used to be that when I heard of people being victimised by romance fraudsters, I'd wonder why they fell for it.' The tea was the perfect temperature now. She sighed with contentment as she took a long drink.

'I was the very same – until yesterday.' Peggy's hair was gelled into submission, so it hardly moved when she shook her head. 'Honestly. I thought the victims should have known better—'

Madge wagged a finger. 'No, these operations are sophisticated. And they specifically target people at their most vulnerable. Most people would be shocked by how professional they've become. They know the right amounts to evade detection and they coach their victims on what to say when questioned.'

'That's what I was going to say.' Baz felt a little rush of adrenaline. 'I know about romance scams because of my work with the police. I investigated a few crime rings in my time.'

Baz had trained as a forensic accountant and worked as a civilian investigator focused on financial crimes during her career with the RCMP. 'But, I'm curious, Madge. You seem to have a much better understanding than most people outside the world of finance. Did you—' She bit off the rest of her question when she realised how rude it was.

'Me?' Madge smoothed the sleeve of the teal jumper she was knitting and studied it. 'Not directly, no. From Cheryl.'

Baz opened her mouth to ask whether Madge's daughter had been targeted but Madge waved her unspoken question away.

'No, she wasn't a victim. A close friend of hers was, though. And that inspired Cheryl to put her professional experience to work in setting up a support group for victims. She's been running it for, hmm…' Madge tapped her lip. 'I want to say it's been almost five years now.'

'Her professional experience?' Baz didn't know what Cheryl did for a living. They'd met once in passing – but she didn't know much about the younger woman.

'Cheryl's the only one of my kids who chose to follow me into nursing.' The gleam in Madge's eye spoke of an intense pride. 'Her daughter too. Zoe's still on maternity leave. Layla's six months old now, so she'll be going back to work in the next week or so.'

Peggy didn't look up from her laptop. 'I'm pretty sure we're not so uncivilised in this country as to force new mothers back to work so soon.'

A broad grin split Madge's face as she waved a hand in Peggy's direction. 'Oh, you'll like this – very modern. Zoe and David – that's her partner. He's a civil servant. Anyhow, they're splitting the parental leave. She took the first six months and he's taking the rest.'

Peggy nodded. 'Good. More fathers need to be involved like that.'

'Stanley took time off when I had Sarah. It wasn't the done thing back then – but he was such a good man. And an excellent father. All my children had good fathers – even Julie. Man was a terrible boyfriend – but he was always good with Julie. Of course, Winston's father wasn't around – but then I wasn't sure who he was, so…' Madge shrugged.

After a moment, she turned back towards Baz. 'Anyhow… In answer to your question, Cheryl works in mental health. When her friend was the target of one of these rings, she did some research and found it's quite a common thing. So she put her experience to work and established this support group I mentioned. You'd be surprised how many people they get.'

'That's very good of her,' Baz said. 'Maybe Tina could benefit from the support they provide.'

Peggy pulled herself to her feet and gestured for Cookie to stay where he was – under the table. 'She almost certainly would. I very much doubt she'll go for it, but I'll definitely mention it. I'm just off to the loo. Anyone need anything while I'm up?'

They worked in silence for a few minutes but, eventually, Madge continued. 'Cheryl also organises sessions for banks, teaching their frontline staff to spot signs of romance fraud. And she facilitates webinars for the general public on how to protect themselves. I'm surprised she's never tried to rope you in to working with her – all your financial experience could be useful.'

'Oh?' A little thrill ran through Baz at the thought of being able to help people in a tangible way.

'I'm sure that's wonderful.' Peggy squeezed herself behind Madge to return to her chair. 'But what are we going to do about Tina's magically disappearing beau?'

'I've got a few ideas about what we can do.' Carole's face was both terrifying and cheerful as she drew her thumb across her throat.

Baz swallowed. 'Er, I was thinking she should contact her bank.' She bit her lip before continuing. 'I'd be happy to assist with that, of course.'

Peggy scoffed. 'You think a bank is going to just give her her money back?'

'Well, actually,' said Baz, at the same time as Madge said, 'They have...'

Both women apologised and encouraged the other to go first.

Peggy shook her head. 'Oh, for heaven's sake. Baz first, then

Madge.' She pointed a finger tipped with fresh navy-blue nail polish in Baz's direction. 'Go.'

'Sorry,' Baz repeated. 'What I was going to say was that banks have a responsibility to identify and prevent potential fraud. Unless the bank can prove that their customer was involved in the crime, they may have to reimburse fraudulent transactions.'

'Mmm hmm.' Madge wagged a finger at Baz. 'That's exactly it. Julie has helped a few of Cheryl's clients make claims.'

'Julie?' Baz thought that might be another of Madge's family members. 'Your sister?'

Madge shook her head. 'You're thinking of Jackie. She lives in Chester. Retired GP. No, Julie is my eldest.'

Sarah ducked into the room with a tray of everyone's second orders. She looked frazzled as she set the drinks out on the table. 'I think that's everything.'

'Are you all right, Sarah?'

Sarah turned to Baz with a smile – though it was a tired one. 'Sorry. Olena's just told me she's got a new job. I've no idea what I'll do without her. I'm run off my feet as it is. I'll need to get someone else in to help out.'

'Oh, I'm sorry,' Baz said. 'Olena's lovely. She's been training as a paramedic – hasn't she?'

Sarah stacked the dirty dishes on the same tray. 'Yeah. That's what she's going to be doing. I'm happy for her – just feeling sorry for myself, I suppose. I don't relish the idea of starting the recruitment process all over again. Anyhow, I should get back.' Balancing the loaded tray on one hand, she touched Baz on the shoulder before returning to the café's main room.

When she was gone, Baz looked back at Madge. 'I don't think I've met Julie.'

Madge chuckled. 'I dare say you've not met half my brood.

Sarah, obviously. You've met Cheryl, haven't you? And Winston, I think? Anyhow, Julie and her partner live in Brighton. They're both lawyers.'

Peggy tossed her second espresso back. 'If we've finished with today's genealogy report, I vote we talk about what we can do about this miscreant. There's no way Tina's his only victim. We need to put a stop to his activities.'

'I've got some ideas.' Carole repeated, proudly hefting her embroidery work so everyone in the room could see the gory scene she was working on.

Baz's stomach fluttered. 'I think we should try the bank first.'

'Besides,' Madge added. 'The vast majority of these scams originate overseas. I don't mind delivering up a bit of justice – but my Oyster card doesn't get me past zone 6.'

'I thought the zones went up higher than that now?' At a look from Peggy, Baz wished she hadn't spoken. 'Sorry. Not the point.'

'I'm not so sure,' Peggy said. 'From what Tina told me, this Steve had a lot of local knowledge – not just the stuff someone could see on Google Maps. Things only a true local would know. So, at the very least, this person or group has a local connection.'

wherein baz contemplates the effects of nature and nurture

THE FOLLOWING MORNING, Baz and her friends had just settled in with their drinks when the bell above the door sounded. She'd recently noticed that both Peggy and Madge did the same – it was just somehow more subtle when they did it.

And Carole never missed a thing. She might seem to be away with the fairies, but she had an eagle eye.

The newest entrant to the café was someone they knew – though, to be fair, there weren't many locals the ladies didn't know. Madge was the social butterfly of the group, but they were all fairly well acquainted with people in the community.

'Good morning, Jimi!' She waved at him.

Her new tenant was wearing a beautiful orange shirt emblazoned with embroidery in a whole rainbow of colours. He smiled broadly when he spotted the women. 'Ah, beautiful ladies of the coffee shop. Good morning. Please excuse me for a moment while I place my order. I'll be right back.'

The women returned to their respective drinks and crafts. 'Look what I've got.' Baz pulled a red rubber thimble from her pocket.

Peggy chuckled. 'Good to see you'll not be stabbing yourself anymore – or at least not quite so frequently.' Over her drainpipe jeans, she wore a black T-shirt with the words 'Skunk Anansie' and some abstract, though vaguely insectoid, artwork. Baz assumed it was a band, though it wasn't one she was familiar with.

Madge peered over her glasses at the new thimble Baz was holding up for her friends to see. 'Oh, you managed to replace your supplies? Or just this?' In contrast to Peggy's attire, Madge wore a floral-patterned top in what appeared to be a soft, stretchy cotton.

Baz hefted her craft bag onto her lap and began removing the contents she'd need for the morning's session. 'No, I've got all sorts – new hoops, threads, needles, and all the various accoutrements I'll need. Everything was delivered yesterday with the thimble. Oh, and I got some lovely new patterns.'

She looked over at Carole. 'Inspired by your artwork, I've even opted for some more ... subversive pieces. And I'm so grateful for your loan – I'll return everything I borrowed.'

Carole looked out the window as she replied. 'Good artists borrow – great ones steal.' She was wearing a sweatshirt emblazoned with creepy doll faces, over the top of leopard-print leggings.

'I should finish with the sweary bird print today.' Baz pulled out the package of supplies. 'Would you like the framed piece when I'm done with it?' She made to hand the package to Carole.

Carole reached out and swiped the bundle out of Baz's outstretched hand with a cheeky grin. But instead of putting it into her bag, she tossed it across the café. 'What did I just tell you, woman?'

As much as Baz was horrified at Carole's rejection of her

offering, a little thrill went through her at being addressed as 'woman'.

From the doorway between the café's two rooms, Jimi let out a small cough. He seemed to have caught the little parcel. It must have been quite a deft manoeuvre. For one thing, Madge was applauding and Peggy whistled. For another, he held a takeaway coffee in one hand and a plate of pastries in the other. Somehow, he'd managed to trap the little bundle between the plate and the mug. 'Careful, you ladies are going to give me a heart attack.'

'Bravo, Jimi. Neatly done.' Baz turned back to Carole. 'If you're certain you don't want the supplies I borrowed—'

'Stole.' Carole's smile was cheerful but insistent.

Jimi set the plate of pastries and the coffee on the table before turning to drag another chair from across the room.

There was no winning with Carole. If she preferred one word over another, that's all there was to it. 'If you're certain you don't want the supplies I *stole*' – Carole looked pleased as she nodded – 'then I shall keep them.'

Jimi set his chair between Madge and Baz, partially blocking the door.

'We'll make a proper criminal out of you yet.' Carole put another stitch in her embroidery and then studied the gory scene on her lap. 'I couldn't be more proud.'

Baz swallowed. She didn't like to think about such things – especially when you factored in the activities the women sometimes got up to. 'If that's what you want, I promise to put the supplies to good use. Thank you.'

'Good morning, Jimi.' Madge patted the man's knee.

Jimi shuffled his chair forwards, pulling closer to the table. 'I brought some delicious treats for you beautiful ladies.' He waved a hand at the plate of goodies. 'Please help yourselves.'

'Thank you, Jimi.' Baz didn't want to be the first one to help herself – but the almond croissant was just begging to be eaten. She gripped her embroidery tighter to prevent her hands from accidentally wandering.

'That's very kind of you, Jimi.' Madge put a hand on his knee before reaching out and helping herself to a cinnamon brioche.

Baz reached for the almond croissant at the same time as Peggy did. 'Sorry, Peggy. Please go ahead.'

'Oh, I wouldn't dream of taking your croissant.' Peggy took her hand back and gestured for Baz to go first. 'Go right ahead. I was reaching past it for the pain aux raisins. Carole, my love, there's a mushroom croissant with your name on it.'

Carole had turned so she was facing the window. 'My name is not Linda or Susan or Caroline or Marjorie or Avril or anything else you want to call me.'

Peggy put the two pastries on separate serviettes and handed one to Carole. 'I know, my love. The names aren't literally on them. I only meant that our friend here seems to have asked Sarah about our preferences.' She raised her pastry like one would a glass and thanked Jimi for the goodies.

'I confess that is exactly what I did.' Jimi helped himself to the one remaining item on the plate – a puff pastry Baz was pretty sure was stuffed with assorted veg. He took a little bite. 'Mmm! Delicious.'

Madge touched his knee again. 'To what do we owe the pleasure of both your company and your generosity?'

The edges of his mouth gradually crept outwards until he wore a broad grin. 'Why can I not give my wonderful friends a little treat?'

Lifting her hand off his knee, Madge waved at him playfully. 'Oh, we're very open to sweet-talking by charming, handsome men.'

Peggy gave an unsubtle cough.

'Pay no heed to my friend. *Some* of us enjoy the company of men very much.' Was Madge actually batting her eyelashes? 'But the fact remains... I would like to know if this flattery is of a business or personal nature.'

Jimi lifted his hands – one still clutching his coffee and the other the remnants of his pastry. 'Why can it not be both? Beautiful women deserve to be treated as queens – in business and in pleasure. I wanted to see you again. And I *also* wanted to remind you of my offer in regard to my business.'

Madge nodded, seeming satisfied with his answer.

The bell above the door tinkled again and Baz turned to spy a tall, thin White woman walk in, carrying a hefty backpack, lugging a bright red suitcase, and wearing a baby strapped to her chest. She waved at the front counter, calling out to Sarah, before turning and ducking through the entrance into the second room.

Her long blond hair was pulled back in a messy bun and she wore blue capri trousers and a chunky red necklace. Baz would have guessed she was around forty years old – though she knew the woman's actual age was a few years north of that figure.

'Morning, all. How's everyone keeping?' She squeezed past Jimi with some effort as he pulled his chair as close to Madge as he could. 'Oh my days! Sorry I'm late. What a palaver the trains were this morning. I should've been here half an hour ago.' She shoved her suitcase up against the wall and dumped her backpack unceremoniously atop it. 'Hello there. Aren't you a tall drink of water. How do you know my mother? And what are your intentions with her?'

With a puzzled look on his face, Jimi pulled himself to his feet and motioned for her to sit. As she did so, his eyes roamed around the group questioningly. After a moment, he waved a hand at Peggy – as though suggesting this might be her daughter.

Peggy responded with an indecorous snort. 'Not a chance, mate!' She looked over at Cheryl. 'No offence. Any mother would be lucky to have you. But I ain't *anybody's* mother.' She wagged a finger.

Jimi looked confused again. He glanced from Baz to Carole and then back again.

'That's all right, dear,' Madge replied. 'At least you messaged me with an updated time. Jimi, this is my daughter Cheryl – and the baby is Layla.' The baby was curled up against Cheryl's chest, with her chubby little pink feet poking out the sides of her sling.

Jimi's confusion vanished as soon as it had arrived. 'Ah, of course! I see it now – you're the spitting image of your sister. How lovely to make your acquaintance. I'm Olujimi Adewale, proprietor of the new bookshop on the broadway.'

Cheryl smiled warmly. 'Oh, I do love a good book. Great to meet you, Olujimi.'

Cookie finally woke up and noticed the newcomer. He pulled himself out from under the table, on his elbows, before standing up and greeting Cheryl enthusiastically, leaning against her and swishing his tail every which way. The baby, who had been sleeping soundly, woke when Cookie licked her bare toes.

Madge coughed. 'That's Mr Adewale to you.'

Cheryl looked down her nose at her mother in an expression that was pure Madge – sass all the way. 'It's very nice to meet you, Mr Adewale. It's always nice to meet one of Mum's *friends*.' She winked at the man in a way that left little to the imagination.

He took both her hands in his and told her it was his pleasure – then touched the baby gently on the nose. Fishing another of his leaflets from his pocket, he encouraged Cheryl to stop by his shop, before wishing everyone a good day and leaving the café.

Madge and Cheryl looked at each other. Both women immediately cracked up – hooting and howling with laughter. The baby joined in the giggling, squealing with delight.

Baz couldn't help but grin as she waved at the baby. What an adorable face she had – and such striking grey eyes.

Peggy glanced over at Baz and shook her head. It didn't feel like a 'no, don't say anything' – more like a shared moment of gentle humour.

After a few moments, Cheryl slapped her knees and stood back up. 'Right, I should go pl— Oh! Well done, sis. You saved me a trip to the counter.'

'Extra hot – just the way you like it.' Sarah set the mug on the table and hugged her sister – the baby contentedly squished between them. As Baz looked at the two younger women, she noticed how physically similar they were. Cheryl was older and had straight blond hair and alabaster skin, whereas Sarah had curly hair and brown skin. And Cheryl was several inches taller. Okay, maybe they weren't actually that similar at all.

Except for those grey eyes. They had the same eyes.

Sarah squeezed her sister's elbow before releasing her. 'I'd better get back to it.'

'You and the boys are coming to Mum's for dinner tonight, right?'

'Wouldn't miss it.' Sarah ducked back through the doorway.

'It's good to meet you properly, Cheryl.' Baz tickled the baby's pudgy little foot before shaking Cheryl's hand.

'It's Baz, right?'

Madge coughed.

'Sorry, *Ms Spencer*.' Cheryl's handshake was warm but uncomfortably firm. 'Mum talks about you all the time, so I'm looking forward to getting to know you over the next few days.'

'Likewise.' Baz liked this woman already. 'And I take it this is your daughter?'

Cheryl's laugh was as explosive as it was infectious. 'Daughter? Oh, hell no! My baby's housetrained and out of my hair. Zoe's a nurse in her own right.' She stroked the baby's cheeks. 'Layla's my granddaughter.' She held her hands up. 'Now don't tell me I'm not old enough to be a grandmother. There are days when I don't feel old enough and days when I feel older than God.' She laughed again, her voice booming but warm.

Cheryl settled again and slapped the arms of her chair. 'So. What's all this about Tina then, eh? And how can I help?' She picked the mug up off the table – a large mocha by the look of it – and took a long drink, letting out a satisfied groan.

'Well.' Peggy took another bite of her pastry, which was still mostly intact. 'What has your mother told you so far?'

Cookie lay back down again. His tail continued to wag, tickling Baz's toes through her sandals.

'Let's see.' Cheryl set the mug – already half drained – back on the table. 'Romance fraudster. Several thousand pounds. Disappeared after she made a very sensible phone call. Anything else?'

'Of course, we know the truth.' Carole looked Cheryl dead in the eye. 'It's all religious propaganda designed to make us look bad. They want the world to hate us even more than they already do, so they send their thugs and charlatans in to do their dirty work. Just like a Bloody Mary – it's all tomato purée, Worcestershire sauce, and red wine. Then they point at us and say it was all our idea. It's beyond disgusting.'

Peggy touched a fingertip to her lips. The nail polish had been refreshed again overnight – it was a sort of slime green now. 'The bit that's missing is the local angle – this villain defi-nitely knows the local community.'

Cheryl leant forwards at that. 'Local angle?' If she were a

dog, Baz was certain her ears would be standing straight up. 'Mum, you didn't mention any local angle. What's this?'

'Of course I did. Why would I leave that part out?' Madge glared at her daughter.

'If you'd mentioned a local angle, I would definitely have remembered it.' Cheryl unwrapped the sling and turned the baby around to face the room.

Madge kissed her teeth. 'I told you the man was local—'

Cheryl kissed her teeth right back. 'You told me he *said* he was local to Tina, not that—'

'Exactly!' Madge carried on knitting without looking up. 'I said he was loc—'

'There's a huge difference between claiming to be local and actually having specific local knowl—'

'Enough!' Peggy barked the word with sufficient authority that both Madge and her daughter were immediately silenced. Everyone in the room – including the baby and several patrons at other tables – turned to look at her. 'It doesn't matter who said what to whom. Cheryl's here now and we can fill her in on the details.'

'Too right.' Madge and Cheryl not only spoke in unison, but they also nodded at precisely the same time and in the same curt way.

Carole looked up. 'Good to see you, Chez. When did you get here?'

'Hi, Mrs Ballard.' Cheryl nodded at Carole. 'Not long. How are you, love?'

Carole's smile gave Baz goosebumps. 'Did I tell you I got a new rolling pin?'

'So.' Peggy fixed Madge and Cheryl with a stare that said very clearly not to interrupt. 'As I was saying, Tina's got a very logical mind. Yes, she can be a bit vulnerable in some ways – but she's incredibly pragmatic. This man was able to convince her he was local. That took more than things he could look up on Google Maps.'

Cheryl pursed her lips and considered this. 'Do you have any examples? What sorts of local knowledge are we talking?' The baby turned herself around and clambered up on her grandmother's lap. She grabbed hold of Cheryl's chunky necklace and popped one of the beads straight into her mouth.

Baz raised a hand and opened her mouth to point out what was happening, but Cheryl waved her off. 'It's designed for that. I think Layla's about to cut her first teeth, so I came prepared. She's been gnawing on it the whole way here.'

Peggy looked up at the ceiling for a moment before answering Cheryl's question. 'Let's see, I know she mentioned that he knew Richard – the developmentally disabled man who works in Deptford Market and will always stop to pet every dog that passes. I think she said he knew the original location of Little Nan's Bar. You remember – when it was just around the corner from here, through the door with the ancient Tory logo?'

'On Deptford Broadway.' Cheryl picked up her mug again. 'Of course I remember – that's where Sarah first met Sam.'

'You're right! I forgot all about that.' Madge reached over and plucked her great-granddaughter from Cheryl's lap, cooing at her.

Cheryl drained the rest of her coffee in one go then set the mug back down. 'You want to hear something funny?' She wagged a finger. 'Not funny ha ha. Funny strange.'

Baz and the others all looked at her.

'I've had multiple clients in the last two months that have been targeted by someone with strong local ties. One of them' – she raised her hands in self-defence – 'even told me he'd mentioned "the little old ladies" who meet at the coffee shop every morning.'

CHAPTER 6

in which peggy struggles to parse textspeak

IT WAS a little after midnight when Peggy's phone buzzed with an incoming text. She'd always been a night owl, so it didn't bother her. But most of her friends tended in the other direction. Even Carole had retired to bed almost an hour ago. With a grunt, she shifted her computer off her lap and leant forwards to retrieve her phone.

Squinting, she held the device at arm's length. She did *not* need glasses – her vision had always been perfect, thank you very much.

NEW NUMBER

hi hi my names Suzy got ur number from
Chezza down the Cominty Centre 😂 she says
UR lookin at the scum Steve what broke my
<3 an run off wiv my 👗 hope you get the
w⚓ lemme know f u wona tak 👍💚

sorry 2 msg so l8 🍷 🍷 🍷 🍷 hope i din
wake u ⏰

Peggy stared at the message for an age. 'Maybe I do need

glasses.' She turned the screen towards Cookie. He sniffed the phone, then cocked his head.

'You can't make heads or tails of this mess either, eh?'

Seemingly satisfied that the device was not, in fact, made of cheese, the dog turned around and returned to his chair. He clambered up on it, turned around three times – very carefully – then lay down and went to sleep.

Peggy shook her head. She pressed the button to place the call.

'Hello?'

'Is this Suzy?'

After the incoherent mess of her text messages, Peggy wasn't sure what to expect from the woman on the other end of the line – but Suzy was surprisingly articulate.

'That's me. Are you Peggy?'

'I am – and please don't worry about messaging so late. I haven't been to bed before midnight since 1972.'

Suzy laughed at that and there was a brief lull in the conversation. Unlike most people from her generation, Peggy hated talking on the phone. Without visual cues, she was never sure whose turn it was to talk. And good luck figuring out the other party's state of mind. 'First of all, Suzy, I want to thank you for agreeing to talk to me. I know this must be a very difficult topic for you and I want to assure you that—'

A strangled sort of noise burst out of Suzy. It took a moment before Peggy realised the woman was laughing – and then it was a few more seconds before Suzy caught her breath enough to respond. 'Sorry, hun. You don't gotta tiptoe around the issue with me. I've moved past all the shame and guilt and all that nonsense.'

Peggy nodded. 'Good. It's important—'

'Yeah. Now I'm all about the anger. Pure rage, you know

what I mean? I want him to pay. My bank helped me get some of my money back. But that bastard needs to be taught a lesson.' Judging by her voice and accent, Peggy estimated Suzy as somewhere in her fifties. Local. White. Probably working class.

'I'm sure—'

'He took me for almost four hundred quid. That might not sound like much to someone like— Well, I mean it might not sound like a lot to some people. But I'm on a low income – pay cheque to pay cheque, you get me? Before Chezza helped me talk to the bank, I thought—'

When Suzy cut herself off mid-sentence, Peggy tried to get a word in. 'I'm so sorry you—'

'I genuinely thought I was going to end up on the streets. I got behind on my rent. For a couple of weeks, the only times I had anything to eat was when I was at the pub. Where I work, I mean. We get discounts on food but sometimes we get freebies – like if someone returns a dish or if there's leftovers at the end of the night. And for two weeks that was all I ate. The free stuff, you know? I didn't have a single quid, so I couldn't buy nuffink.'

Peggy let the silence hang for just a moment to see if Suzy would keep talking. When she didn't, Peggy said, 'I'm so sorry. You didn't deserve that. That sounds terrible. And none of it was your fault.'

Suzy barked out a laugh. 'Oh, I know that. Don't you worry. I was only trying to set the scene for you. I want you to understand why I'm so angry. And why I'm ready to do whatever it takes to help you find that monster.'

Peggy nodded approvingly – not that Suzy could see her.

'Maybe put him outta my misery if you get me.' Peggy opened her mouth to respond, but Suzy clarified. 'Only joking, sis. Or maybe talking metaphorically, I mean. I'd never do real violence – even though I might feel like it, if you know what I mean.'

'Understood. My friends and I are grateful for your support in this.' Peggy ran a hand along the threadbare velour of her sofa. 'But I'd like to ask you a few questions if I may – because I want to be sure we're talking about the same scoundrel.'

'Ask away.' Suzy made a bring-it-on gesture along with the words – or at least she did in Peggy's mental picture of the woman.

'Thank you.' Peggy touched her face before continuing. 'How did you meet this Steve?' The name itself could be a coincidence, especially since it almost certainly wasn't his real name.

'He messaged me on Facebook. We was both part of the same group in Facebook – one for residents of Deptford and New Cross.' She paused for just a second. 'You know *sarf-ees* London, right?'

Peggy nodded then remembered the woman couldn't see her. She couldn't keep a chuckle out of her voice. 'I've been living in Deptford since 1979.'

'Right, so anyhow, this guy DM'd me. Said he'd read my comments on a couple a posts – nothing creepy-like. Just general stuff about the area – like the group went absolutely bonkers about every time Royal Tea announced a new show. You probably never heard of them – they're a local drag act. Great fun. Oh, and Little Nan's Bar. That group loves Little Nan's. But who doesn't – am I right?'

Peggy was going to say she did indeed know Blue and Ron, the couple behind Royal Tea. And that Little Nan's was indeed a lovely establishment. Tristan, the proprietor, was a fine young man.

But Suzy was on a roll. 'So, as the kids say, he slides into my DMs. All sweetness and whatnot. He was originally from

America but he done a contract in London last year and he was looking to make his home here as soon as his current contract ended. Pure BS in hindsight, of course. But at the time, it felt like he really got me – like he saw the real me. He said I was beautiful. Do you even know how long it's been since somebody called me beautiful?'

Peggy wouldn't have known how to answer that even if Suzy had left a gap in her speech. She heard liquid sloshing around in a glass as the woman spoke – and who could blame her? Peggy reached across to the side table and picked up her own glass. She took a long drink while Suzy continued.

'Far too long – that's how long. He told me he'd been recently divorced and that he wasn't enjoying being alone. I told him I'd been alone since my Roger died. It was Covid that got him in the end. Well, they said it was his heart. Maybe it was both. He'd always had a bit of a bum ticker. He died on Christmas Day in 2020. Put me right off Christmas forever – I can tell you that for nothing. Anyhow, I've been on my own ever since and...'

It was a few seconds before Peggy realised Suzy had actually stopped talking rather than having paused to take a breath.

'I'm so sorry.' Peggy didn't know what else to say. How could anyone understand another person's grief? She'd nearly lost Carole around that same time – she'd never been more frightened in her life.

The following morning, Peggy met up with her friends at Wellbeloved as usual. Cheryl and the baby were there too. Cheryl's hair had been put into a series of Dutch plaits that looked like they would have been a faff to do but which would be eminently practical to wear.

Peggy was in the process of telling her friends about her late-night conversation with Suzy, when Sarah came in to drop off their drinks.

'Were you talking about romance fraud?' She set the tray down on the small table and set about unloading the various teapots, cups, milk pots, and cutlery.

Madge used her knitting needle to motion towards Carole. 'After young Tina fell prey to someone—'

Carole made a deadly sort of gesture. 'I have some ideas for how we could deal with the perpetrator.'

Madge inhaled sharply as she motioned at Cheryl. 'And then Cheryl put us in touch with some people from her support group who've experienced similar.'

Sarah stood back upright and let the tray hang loose. 'It's funny you should mention it. You remember Debs from the childcare centre? A few weeks back, she told me about a friend of hers who was recently scammed out of almost a thousand pounds. As if anyone has that kind of money to spare. So cruel.' She shook her head.

Peggy pursed her lips. 'It wasn't someone local by any chance, was it?'

'Local? Debs' friend, you mean?' Sarah paused to grab some used dishes from neighbouring tables, stacking them on her tray. 'Yeah, I'm pretty sure he lives around here. Why? Are you thinking to go talk to him?'

Madge wagged a finger at her youngest daughter. 'No, Peggy meant to ask whether the scammer was local – or claimed to be, at any rate.'

Sarah paused on her way back to the main room and put a hand on the stone wall. 'It's funny you should say that. I know these scams mostly originate overseas but Debs said her friend is absolutely convinced this person has some connection to the area. Next time she comes in, I'll ask her to come talk to you. Anyway, back to work I go. Holler if you need anything.'

Peggy raised her eyebrows as she looked at Madge. 'Looks like we're going to need to talk to this friend of Debs.'

'Mmm hmm.' Madge didn't look up from her knitting. 'Sarah will put us in touch with this fellow. Now, Baz, have you heard from your contact since we last spoke?'

Cheryl had told them she had five people in her support group who might have been victimised by the same person. For privacy reasons, she obviously couldn't give out their details. Instead, she spoke to the five and said that some concerned citizens were looking into the cases. She divvied up the contact details so that the calls – if they came – would be spread out amongst the women. Cheryl told her group that, if they felt comfortable doing so, they could contact the name provided to discuss what had happened.

Baz cleared her throat. 'Actually, I heard from a lovely woman last night. We spoke for quite a while.'

Interesting. Peggy had assumed that Baz's anxious demeanour this morning was a sign she'd been talking to that no-good ex-husband of hers. Peggy had never met this Hari, but anyone who could dump a person after thirty years purely because they revealed a truth about themself wasn't a good person in Peggy's mind.

'Bea.' Baz set her embroidery down in her lap. 'That's her name – the woman I spoke to. Anyways, Bea said that she was first contacted by Steve about three months ago.'

'Aw, Bea's lovely.' Cheryl undid the sling wrap and lifted Layla out.

Peggy ran some sums in her head. 'Three months? I think that makes the timeline similar to both Suzy and Tina.'

'Mmm.' It sounded like Madge had come to a similar conclusion. She beckoned for Cheryl to pass the baby to her.

'Was the initial contact on Facebook?' Peggy wondered whether there might be a clue in how the marks were being approached.

Baz smiled at the baby before dragging her eyes in Peggy's

direction. 'Bea told me he first contacted her on Insta. He replied to one of her posts about the services at the local library – that's Peckham, I think she said. That's not far from here, right? I've been back for more than a year and I still get confused.'

'London geography isn't for the faint of heart,' Peggy said. 'London – never "the City" because that's something different – is made up of thirty-two boroughs. Deptford and New Cross are both part of Lewisham. You're with me so far, right?' When Baz nodded, she continued. 'If you walked across New Cross and came out the other side you'd be in Peckham. That's part of Southwark, the next borough over. And, of course, both Lewisham and Southwark are classed as inner London boroughs.'

'Wasn't Deptford its own borough at some point?' Cheryl picked up her coffee mug and drained the last half of her coffee.

The baby fussed a bit on Madge's lap, so she jiggled her. 'Mmm hmm. When we were all children.' She elbowed her daughter. 'Well, all of us except you.'

Baz worried at her embroidery, smoothed her skirt, and tapped her foot. Peggy wondered whether she was aware of how anxious she seemed.

Peggy nodded. 'Of course, if you go back far enough in time, before Deptford was absorbed into London, it was part of Kent.' When she'd let Baz squirm long enough, she waved a hand. 'Sorry, Baz. You were saying?'

Baz gave a small smile. 'Bea's relationship with Steve lasted until six weeks ago. In the time they were together – well, so to speak – he conned her out of quite a bit of money. She wouldn't say how much, but I gather it was a lot.'

Madge inhaled sharply. 'Poor woman.'

Peggy tapped her nails on the arm of her chair. 'I hope she's sought help from her bank.'

Baz cringed. 'I tried to persuade her but I think she's too embarrassed to do so. Bea isn't even her real name. She's filled with so much shame over this.'

'Mmm hmm.' With her mother entertaining the baby, Cheryl had pulled a mountain of knitting from a bag, and she kept her hands busy as she spoke. 'She wears a face mask in group too – I'm all for infection control but, in Bea's case, I think it's more about not wanting anyone to see her. I suspect it took all the spoons she had just—'

Peggy frowned. 'Spoons? What do spoons have to do with it?'

'Sorry.' Cheryl waved a knitting needle apologetically. 'Spoon theory. It's a way of describing how much energy – physical or mental – that a person has available. You start a day with so many and everything that happens adds or removes from your available energy reserves. Or spoons. Anyhow, it took all Bea's spoons to make herself join us. I'm so proud of her for seeking help.'

Baz looked at Cheryl. When Cheryl gave a small wave of her hand, Baz continued. 'She's such a dear. And as with Peggy's person, she's convinced he's local. Or rather, he's been living locally for a few years – enough time to garner plenty of local knowledge. He's fifty-five. American by birth. He told her he'd been away working on an oil rig for the past six months. Same name, similar story – just a different job. But it's really starting to sound like it's all the work of one person.'

Cheryl waved her knitting at Baz. 'Or a group – could be a group. But otherwise, I agree. There are too many coincidences. The timing and the degree of local knowledge. Usually, they're much more vague about their connection to the local area. They'll claim to be from a nearby city or they're from overseas but are looking to move to your city. This degree of local knowledge is weird. Oh, and they're all called Steve.'

'Stephen Wright, in fact,' Baz added.

Madge placed a kiss on the baby's head. 'Is that all, Baz?'

Baz nodded. 'I think so, yes.'

There was a twinkle in Madge's eye as she looked around the room at her friends. 'As it happens, I also spoke to someone last night.'

Cheryl looked at her mother. 'You what, Mum? When was this?'

Madge gave the merest hint of a shrug and a sly grin. 'Anyhow, you lot are *not* going to believe who called me.'

'I'm assuming it was either Mitch or Claire.' Cheryl gave a confused shake of her head. 'They're the only ones I gave your number to.'

Peggy almost dropped her computer on the floor. Baz fumbled her teacup, sloshing liquid over her dress. 'What?'

Carole clapped delightedly. 'If it isn't Mr Gays Against Groomers himself! How the devil is he – does he still play the game of magenta?'

in which baz reveals the story of how she met her husband

BAZ COULDN'T BELIEVE her ears. Fortunately, the tea had cooled somewhat. It was only warm, not scalding. Still, she pulled herself to her feet to go get cleaned up.

Mitch! Or to give him his full name: Crispin Caspian Todd-Mitchell.

She excused herself past the queue and went to grab a stack of serviettes. Sarah spotted her and handed her a damp cleaning cloth instead. Baz patted herself down as she made her way back to the café's second room.

When she lowered herself back into her chair, Cheryl looked at her. 'Mum tells me you lot know Mitch?'

Baz dabbed her tea-soaked dress with the cloth as best she could. She'd have to get it into the wash as soon as she got home or she'd never get the stain out. 'We do indeed.'

Cheryl crossed her arms over her chest and looked down her nose at Baz. 'All right. Which one of you ladies is going to tell me the story?'

'He's your patient, though.' Baz was wary of putting Cheryl in an awkward position.

Cheryl kissed her teeth. 'He's not my patient – he voluntarily attended one session of a support group I run in my spare time.'

Baz still wasn't sure.

'I can't *give you* any information about him, right? That would be a breach of his confidentiality,' Cheryl said. 'That's the same reason I didn't give you the names or contact details of anyone in my group. I provided five people with *your* details and suggested they might want to contact you to assist in your investigation. One of those people told me point-blank she wouldn't. Three of them chose to contact you. My point is' – she waved a hand at Baz – 'there's nothing to say you can't tell me details about someone. *Your* actions aren't governed by professional standards.'

Baz bobbed her head in response to that.

'He was part of the contingency of Danish Hittites that destroyed Oslo in 2002.' Carole smiled broadly, showing perfectly straight teeth as she pulled her needle, trailing blood red thread, through the embroidery hoop. 'And all because Peggy ran him down while Baz stole his lunch money – the big baby. That's what led to the grand plan, you see. It was after that that they started genetically combining the Hittites and the Mesopotamians. At Oxford, obviously.'

'You ran him down, auntie? But he's so lovely!' Cheryl raised an eyebrow as she turned to Peggy, plucking out the one detail in Carole's tale that was grounded in reality.

Peggy held her hands up as though to say she couldn't deny it – which of course she couldn't. 'Hardly. And he was fine. But lovely he is not.'

'Hang on.' Cheryl held up her index finger. 'Are you the reason he's got a broken foot?'

Peggy waved Cheryl's words away. 'What? No. Of course not. This was six months ago and he wasn't injured at all.'

'Even Peter agreed with us,' Madge added.

'Aunties. Mum.' Cheryl massaged her forehead with the fingers of one hand. 'I'm going to need you to tell me this story in some kind of order.'

Baz licked her lips to moisten them. 'We met Mitch earlier this year at a drag show.'

Peggy scoffed. 'Well, not exactly *at* the show.'

'True.' The baby began to fuss, so Madge pulled a bottle from the bag and offered it to her. 'He and his friends were outside the shows, if you can believe it.'

'Mum!' Cheryl's mouth fell open before she turned her expression into a grin. 'You were at a drag show?'

'Oh, Royal Tea are excellent.' Madge dismissed her daughter's amusement. 'You'd like Blue and Ron – such a lovely couple.'

'What?' Cheryl gave her head a little shake.

Madge put a hand on her daughter's arm. 'You remember Clive, yes?'

Cheryl shook her head. 'Ugh, that man!'

'Yes, well, he came to us for help when a friend of his went missing.' Madge released her daughter's arm.

'What does any of this have to do with drag queens – or with Mitch?' Cheryl's eyebrow shot upwards. 'Is... Is Mitch a drag queen?'

Baz bit her lip to prevent a chuckle escaping.

Madge waved her daughter's question away. 'No – far from it. We met him because he was leading a group of people protesting.'

'Protesting? Protesting what?'

'Drag.' Peggy fixed Cheryl with a stare that would have turned Baz's insides to mush not so long ago. Mind you, as she got to know her friend better, she now understood that the look meant Peggy disapproved of the topic under discussion rather than the person she was speaking to.

'What? Why would a gay man protest against drag queens?' Cheryl inhaled sharply. 'Ah, I take it this was a children's story-hour event?'

Peggy snorted.

Madge shook her head. 'The audience was mostly our age.'

'Your age!' Cheryl scrunched her face up. 'Why on earth – oh, never mind. People confound me.'

'I think,' Baz began. 'I think the gist of it was that the shows were in community centres and libraries where children could conceivably be in the vicinity.'

Peggy narrowed her eyes. 'Is *that* what they were so angry about?'

'I think so?' Baz wasn't entirely sure why that came out as a question – even though she really wasn't sure at all.

'Right.' Cheryl waved the conversation away. 'I'm still going to need you to tell me how Peggy came to assault the man.'

'Sweet? Ha! He was being aggressive – threatening Baz.' Peggy raised her hands. 'I ... may have ... accidentally depressed my mobility scooter's accelerator instead of the brake.'

Cheryl's jaw hung open. 'Threatening Baz? In that case, I'm surprised that's all you did.'

Peggy raised her shoulders and eyebrows.

Madge slapped her daughter's arm. 'Man fell on his arse!' She was overcome with giggles – much to the delight of Layla the baby. 'Started bellowing for the cops to arrest Peggy. But of course, the cop in question was Peter. He sent Mitch and his gang on their merry way.'

Cheryl reached a hand across to Baz. 'I'm sorry he was abusive to you.' She shook her head. 'If I'd known that, I'd never have let him in our group. One of our regular members is trans. I'd never knowingly expose her to potential harm. As luck would have it, though, he was perfectly lovely in group.'

'And now he's been the victim of romance fraud.' Peggy yawned. 'Excuse me. Sorry. Please don't take that as me not caring about a victim – it's just that I was up even later than normal last night.'

'You're excused,' said Madge.

'So?' Peggy let the word linger in the air for a while – presumably hoping that Madge would pick up the story. But Madge was busy fussing at the baby.

Cheryl used her knitting needle to prod her mother. 'I think your friends are waiting for you to tell them what Mitch told you.'

Madge looked up. 'Sorry. Pour me some more tea – would you, Chez?' Cheryl set her knitting down on her lap and bent forwards to do her mother's bidding. 'Mitch rang me last night and said he'd heard I was looking into a local romance fraud-ster. At first, I wondered how he'd heard about our investiga-tion – not to mention how he'd got my number. Imagine my surprise when he told me he'd been targeted as well.'

Peggy tapped her lip pensively. 'Did he know who you were?'

The thought of encountering Mitch again made Baz's insides turn inside out. She'd seen him around the neighbour-hood every so often. None of the women had had any direct contact, though.

A wave of gratitude washed over her that it had been Madge's number he'd been given. Pure luck of the draw, of course – Cheryl had no idea that the gang knew Mitch. But Baz struggled to think how she would have responded if she'd picked up the phone only to find him on the other end of the line.

Chuckling, Madge wagged a finger. 'Not at first, I don't think. But he got there pretty swiftly.'

'I imagine his attitude changed once he figured it out,' Peggy said.

Madge bobbed her head. 'You'd think – but surprisingly not. He was very cordial. Apologetic, even.'

Baz stabbed her finger – she could feel it even through the rubber thimble. 'He what?' Thankfully no blood. The thimble did its job.

Peggy didn't say a word, just cocked an eyebrow.

'I'm not kidding. He said he was very sorry for getting involved with the group that organised those protests.'

Baz almost asked whether he'd mentioned the whole tax evasion thing before stopping herself. Madge probably didn't want her daughter knowing they'd blackmailed the man.

When the bell above the door rang, Baz's eyes were drawn once again to the newcomer: a familiar middle-aged Black woman wearing dungarees, embroidered with flowers, and a brightly coloured head-wrap. Debs. Instead of heading to the front counter, the woman turned and stepped into the café's second room. 'Good morning, Mrs Dixon. Ladies. I hope I'm not interrupting.'

'Good morning, Debs. No trouble at all.' Madge waved a hand at Cheryl. 'This is my daughter Cheryl. Cheryl, this is Debs. She runs the child minders across the road. And how are my little grandsons doing?'

When Debs smiled, it warmed the whole room. 'George and Henry are both doing well. These days, George is only with us for an hour in the mornings before he heads to school. They're both such lovely boys.'

Without pausing her knitting, Cheryl nodded. 'Good to meet you, Debs.'

'And who's this little one – yours?' Debs waved at the baby on Madge's lap.

'Indirectly speaking,' Cheryl said. 'This is my granddaughter, Layla. I've stolen her from my daughter and her partner for a couple of days to give them a break.'

'It's nice that you're able to do that for them.' As Debs moved, the flowers on her dungarees seemed to dance. 'Are you local?'

'Not far. I live over in Camberwell – I'm a nurse at the Maudsley. I work a five-on, five-off pattern. Mum asked for my help with something this week. I still had three days before I needed to be back at work, so I decided to pop on over for a little visit.'

'Oh, that's nice. I bet it doesn't hurt to get a bit of Madge's cooking while you're here, too, eh?'

Cheryl patted her belly. 'Oh gosh, no. That never hurts. Mind you, my Moses – he's my husband – is another great cook. Even got Mum's seal of approval.'

'Aw, that's nice.' Debs clapped once, like she was trying to corral a group of toddlers. 'Now listen, I can't stay – told Jameel I'd only be gone a minute. Sarah told me you're looking into this con artist. I think she told you about my friend Joe Vaz. Everyone calls him Big Joe. He was a victim of something very similar. I rang him this morning after I spoke to Sarah. He said he'd be happy to talk to you, so I wanted to come by and pass on his details.'

Baz reached out to accept the slip of paper Debs was offering. 'Thank you, Debs. We'll be in touch with him today.'

Debs nodded. 'Thank you. Please – go easy on Big Joe. He's a really good friend, loyal to a fault. He's having such a rough time. Because of his disabilities, he doesn't really get out of the house. I think he'd be pleased to have some company – even if it turns out there's not much you can do for him.'

'Of course.'

'Thanks again. I appreciate anything you can do for Big Joe. He's such a lovely man. He didn't deserve this.' Debs waved at the women and bade them farewell before turning and heading back out.

Madge pulled herself to her feet, still holding on to the baby. 'I'm going to step outside for a moment to give this Big Joe a call.' Baz passed her the bit of paper with his details.

Baz set her embroidery aside. 'Would you like me to hold the baby while you make the call?'

'Thank you.' Madge handed Layla to Baz.

The baby threatened to start fussing, so Baz did her best to distract her – making silly faces and blowing raspberries. Layla appeared to consider this for a moment, hovering on that boundary between crying and laughing. Relief rushed through Baz when the infant started giggling, so she carried on doing what she was doing.

When she glanced up, she caught Cheryl smiling at her. 'Looks like you're a bit of a natural.'

A bittersweet tinge of something undefinable ran through Baz. 'I wouldn't ... I guess ... I suppose ... I don't really have much practice.'

'Oh?' Cheryl cocked her head. 'I thought Mum said you had a son.'

The mixed emotions roiling in Baz's guts were so powerful and yet impossible to pin down. Yet before she thought about what she was doing, she found herself telling more of her story than she had ever shared with her friends. 'Cathy, that's Jason's mum – she and I had a very brief relationship in my teens. We'd broken up well before he was born, though. It was ... acrimonious. She wouldn't let me see my son. At all. I think she figured that if she didn't accept money from me, then I didn't have any parental rights. Especially since she didn't put my name on the birth certificate.'

Baz couldn't bear the look of immense sadness on Cheryl's face – nor the anger evident in Peggy's demeanour – so she kept her focus on the baby, who was still smiling and giggling. 'Eventually, I had to hire a lawyer to sue for joint custody.' She paused to smile at the memory as warmth flooded her system. 'I was successful in being recognised as Jason's … parent.'

Even without looking up, Baz was aware of Madge returning to her seat. 'When Jason was three, I won the right to partial custody. It was a horrible process – I wouldn't wish it on anyone. But I'm so glad I pursued it. Not only did I get to spend time with my son as he was growing up – but if I hadn't gone through with it, I wouldn't have Daisy in my life. Also...'

Heat flooded Baz's cheeks as she finally looked up. 'My lawyer had an intern working with her – a law student doing some summer work in family law. He and I stayed in touch after he returned to university in the autumn. In time, we became great friends. Until...' She looked back down at the baby. 'Ten years later, in 1992, we confessed our feelings to one another. And in 2003, we flew to Toronto to get married.'

Peggy arched an eyebrow. 'How is Hari? Any more late-night conversations?' Something about her expression made Baz think her friend didn't approve of her relationship.

'As it happens, I did spend some time on Zoom with him last night.' Baz looked down at the baby. 'Not all night this time – I managed to get to bed at a decent hour. But it's … nice catching up with him.'

Peggy harrumphed.

'Mmm hmm.' Madge took out her knitting, so she probably wasn't in a rush to take the baby back.

That was completely fine with Baz – holding a baby was

something she didn't get to do very often. 'How did your conversation go?'

'Very well.' Madge unrolled the jumper – or rather the bodice front – she was working on and studied it before picking back up where she'd left off. 'Do you ladies have any plans tomorrow afternoon?'

CHAPTER 8

wherein someone is in for a shock

PEGGY DRIED the last of the lunch dishes and put them away.
She wiped her hands on the towel before hanging it back up.

Around the corner, Carole was in the lounge, singing a
raunchy song about... Peggy wasn't actually sure who or what it
was about. Cookie was watching her, enthralled. Or possibly
bored. It was sometimes hard to tell with him.

Peggy went to Carole and took her in her arms. Carole led
her in an impromptu waltz – a bit of a challenge given the small
size of the room, not to mention how full it was. But it was
good fun. Cookie leapt off his chair and joined them, nipping at
their heels.

They carried on for a few minutes until the door buzzer
sounded. Carole released Peggy and danced over to the speaker
on the wall. 'Good afternoon. You're through to the
Mesopotamian Resistance Network. Can I have today's pass-
word, please?' Cookie ran to the door, barking his fool head off.

The speaker crackled to life but Peggy couldn't make out
the response from across the room. Soon afterwards, the buzz
of the lock-release mechanism sounded.

After a moment, the door creaked open and Madge's voice sounded. 'Hello?'

Peggy rounded the corner to find Cookie absolutely delighted to be the recipient of both Madge and Baz's attention. 'Right,' she said. 'The gang's all here – let's head out.' She already had her boots on, so all she had to do was drop her keys and phone into a lightweight jacket, put Cookie's harness on him, and grab her cane from its hook by the door.

Moments later, the four women – plus Cookie, of course – were heading up Harton Street. It turned out Big Joe lived just a five-minute walk from the women's various flats. Peggy and Carole were probably closest, though Madge wasn't much further.

As they made their way out onto the street, Carole regaled them all with the tale of Ronald Reagan, the American president, who built a secret tunnel from New York to the Vatican in the 1920s.

They turned onto Vanguard and from there onto Friendly Street. It was less than a year since the same four women – minus Cookie – had walked this route on a very different mission. Dispatching the so-called Goldsmiths Groper was the first time all four of them had worked together to plan and carry out a bit of extrajudicial justice.

Sort of. Carole's little spur-of-the moment handiwork with her *special* knitting needles was the first time all four had been present for some vengeance. Though that didn't really count since it wasn't something they'd planned.

Today's mission was very different, even if their destination was nearly on top of a previous one. They were here to interview a lonely old man who'd been duped by some unscrupulous person. Perhaps they could dispense a bit of friendship and kindness – but justice wouldn't be served. Not today anyway.

Cookie may not be the cleverest dog Peggy had ever met –

but even he couldn't fail to notice they were heading towards the dog park. Big Joe's flat was in a block that overlooked it. The small urban park provided a fully fenced-in green space for dogs to run free while their humans had a bit of a natter. Peggy didn't care for the place – too much gossip for her liking. But Daisy took Cookie there at least once a week.

When they arrived at the front entrance, Peggy stepped up and used the ferrule of her cane to press the appropriate buzzer.

'Big Joe said it may take him a minute or two to respond,' Madge said. 'He struggles with his mobility.'

Peggy leant on her cane. 'I think we can all relate to that. Or I certainly can, at any rate.'

Having parked her scooter next to the bins to the left of the entrance, Baz dismounted and joined her friends. 'Ditto for me.'

The intercom system crackled to life. 'Hello? Is that you, Madge?'

Madge stepped up to the speaker. 'It is. And I've brought my friends.'

'Delightful. Come on through. I'm on the first floor. There's a lift if you need it and then I'm just down the hall to the left.' The speaker crackled, missing a syllable here and there – but the buzz of the unlocking mechanism sounded.

Madge stepped in first. Once they'd made it to the first floor, she pointed to a sign on the wall giving directions to the various flat numbers. 'This way.' She walked straight forwards.

The others followed suit. Madge stopped midway along the corridor. A door on the right-hand side stood ajar. 'Knock, knock?'

From somewhere out of sight, a voice answered. 'Come on through, dolls.' A South African accent.

The women and Cookie entered the inner hall. Madge and

Baz stopped to remove their shoes. Peggy couldn't imagine doing that. Her fourteen-hole Doc Martens were a pain in the arse. She put them on in the morning and didn't like removing them until at least dinner time. It's why she tried to avoid going to Madge and Baz's homes – they both generally asked people to remove their shoes.

Peggy had recently replaced the laces with a sneaky zip. But, even so, it was still a pain in the arse putting them on and taking them off again.

Big Joe's home was cluttered and the furniture was threadbare – much like the flat Peggy shared with Carole. Every wall and all the surfaces were adorned with queer artwork. The man himself was heavyset and younger than Peggy had imagined – probably about sixty. He was White, with thick glasses and not much hair. A hose connected to an oxygen tank on one end; the other end terminated in little nose prongs on Big Joe's face. A walker sat next to the plush armchair on which he sat.

'Don't mind me if I don't get up to greet you, ladies. I used to say I was just a bear in trousers – but these days I'm more of a hibernating one. Anyhoo – welcome, welcome. Come on in and make yourselves at home.'

'It's lovely to meet you, Big Joe.' Madge stepped forwards and shook his hand. His nails were tipped with pink glittery polish. 'These are my friends' – she pointed at each woman in turn – 'Baz, Peggy, and Carole.'

The four exchanged greetings. Cookie bounded over to Big Joe, nearly ripping out the man's nasal cannula in his desire to befriend someone new.

She whispered a cringing apology but Big Joe waved her off. 'No harm done. He only wants to be friends. What's his name?' He took Cookie's head in his hands and scratched his ears in just the right way.

'That's Cookie. He can be a bit of an oaf but he means well.'

Social niceties weren't Peggy's forte, so she took the bag of goodies from Madge's hands. 'Shall I make us all a cuppa?'

'Oh, that sounds delightful, if you wouldn't mind.' Big Joe rubbed his hands together. 'My carer has been by this morning, so there should be some clean dishes in the cupboard. It's just through there.' He pointed in the direction of the kitchen. Not that Peggy could have missed it – the flat was even smaller than her own.

As Peggy headed off on her mission, Madge bobbed her head at the oxygen tank. 'COPD?'

Peggy would have had a different guess – but Madge was the nurse.

Big Joe nodded. 'And AIDS.' Ah, there it was. Peggy had been right after all. 'When I tested positive for HIV back in 1988, it was still supposed to be a death sentence.'

Big Joe laughed, which turned into a coughing spell. 'To be fair, it will eventually kill me. But I've outrun old Mrs Death for more than thirty-five years thus far. And I reckon I've still got a few more left in me yet. Not quite ready to join the bleeding choir invisible, me.'

Baz joined Peggy in the poky little kitchen. The window faced the same direction as the main room, giving an excellent view of the dog park across the road. Between the two of them, they filled the kettle, got some mugs and plates down, and set about prepping a mini feast. Madge had brought a loaf cake and Baz had some little Bakewell tartlets. Peggy was certain that either or both of them would have had a stash of teabags and possibly milk – just in case Big Joe hadn't had them on hand. But he had plenty.

He even had a jar of instant coffee, so Peggy didn't have to go without. She stacked up plates and mugs while Baz made tea in a commemorative Princess Diana teapot. When they were ready to go, they carried everything through to the main room.

Madge had her stethoscope out and was checking Big Joe's breathing. Sliding the device back into its case, she stood upright. 'A little faster than I'd like, but no crackles.' She patted him on the arm. 'How do you take your tea?'

'Same as I take my men.' Big Joe's eyes sparkled with humour as he pressed pudgy fingers to his lips. 'Any way I can get them, doll! But seriously, though, I'll have about three sugars and as much milk as you can fit into the mug.'

Peggy and Baz arranged the treats on the little coffee table. Baz poured Big Joe his tea, and then placed some goodies on a little plate and brought them over to him.

'Cheers, love. You're a doll.' He took a dainty little bite out of the cake. 'Ooh, lemon drizzle! Mmm, that is divine. Did one of you make this?'

Madge beamed. 'That one was me. Baz made the tartlets.'

Big Joe nodded. 'Well, you ladies can come by any time.' He dabbed his lips with a napkin. 'I'm kidding, of course. You don't need to bring anything at all – but I do love the company.'

He tore a tiny titbit off his cake and handed it to Cookie. At least it was only a small piece. 'I often see you walk this handsome young man past my window. I always wished I could get to know you – and now here you are. And if I'm not mistaken, I see someone else with him at the dog park once or twice a week. A tall young woman with platinum hair. Your granddaughter, I assume, Peggy?'

Peggy barked a laugh. 'I can assure you, I am no one's parent.'

'Nonsense.' Carole was busy piling a tiny plate full of treats. 'You've been Tina's father since Harvey tragically fell in the drink.'

Baz took a seat on the armchair to Big Joe's left. 'Daisy's my granddaughter, actually.'

When everyone had a plate of tasty nibbles and a mug of

something hot, they settled onto whatever seats they could find. Peggy joined Madge on the small sofa across from Big Joe. Carole perched herself on a wheeled stool and amused herself – and Cookie – by spinning around and making whooping noises.

Big Joe peered over the top of his mug. 'Now then, I do love having company. Any excuse for a tea party's a good one in my book. But I believe you actually came here for a purpose, no?'

'We did indeed.' Madge pulled a floral-printed hardback notebook and pen from her handbag. 'As I mentioned yesterday, we're doing a bit of research into a romance fraud targeting people in the local community.'

'Steve,' Big Joe said. The smile was wiped off his face. 'Turns out he was no Mr Right after all, eh?'

Peggy folded her hands in her lap. 'That does seem to be the name he's going by.'

'That absolute ... brigand.' Big Joe covered his mouth with his hand. 'Sorry, ladies. I'm afraid I very nearly said something worse there. But what that man did to me—' He paused to wipe away tears with his sleeve.

Baz leant over the edge of the sofa to pat his knee. 'I'm so sorry, Big Joe. I promise we'll do what we can to find out who did this.' He put his hand over hers, appearing to grip quite hard.

Peggy knocked her coffee back – not bad for instant – and set the mug down on the cluttered coffee table. 'How did you first encounter Steve?'

'Well, now.' Big Joe shifted his position on the chair, before picking his mug back up from the crowded end table next to him. 'I think Debs – and isn't she just the loveliest girl? We've been friends for – oh gosh – it must be around thirty years now. We met back at G-A-Y in the nineties. We became fast friends – quite literally fast. I think I ended up crashing on her sofa from the very night we met. It was because of her that I moved to Deptford. When I moved over from Johannesburg, I first lived way out in Barnet. I'll admit it was the name Cockfosters that drew me there. But that didn't last long. Then I bounced around, here and there. Spent some time at a squat in Camden.'

Peggy was starting to wish she'd brought her laptop. The man was lovely, but he couldn't half talk. If the whole investigation went like this, they'd never get to the bottom of this blasted fraud.

Big Joe waved his words away. 'Sorry, you didn't come to talk about my history – delightfully sordid though it may be.'

He winked at Peggy. 'And I can assure you it was most *definitely* sordid. Anyhoo, what I was trying to say was I think Debs told you that I don't really get out much. Which is to say that I'm what the kids call "extremely online". I spend pretty much all day every day talking to people all over the world. Grindr, Bluesky, Facebook, Mastodon, Reddit, TikTok. Not Twitter anymore, obviously. But if there's a site with queer people, I'm there.'

Peggy had no idea what half those sites were. She was far from a technophobe – but social media really wasn't her thing. Too many people who really seemed to enjoy being angry just for the hell of it. She paid a lovely young woman in Manila to handle her author social media profiles for her.

Big Joe raised his hands in something that wasn't quite a shrug and wasn't quite a flourish, but could have been an approximation of either. 'I've made some wonderful friends over the years. And some ... more than friends.' He batted his eyelashes coyly. 'So when Steve commented on one of my posts on a local Reddit forum... Well, at first I didn't think much of it.'

Madge was scribbling furiously in her notebook – though heaven only knew what she thought was relevant to the case from what he'd told them so far.

Big Joe started tearing up again. Baz leant forwards and touched his knee again.

He clasped her hand in his left while waving his right. 'I'm all right, I'm all right. As I say, Steve commented on one of my Reddit posts – I think it was about the dog park.'

'He said he had a dog?' Peggy leant forwards and rested her weight on her elbows. That matched with what Tina had said.

'No, well, yes, but no. Oh, hark at me getting all tangled up over my words. Never think I used to be a singer, would you? I was. I was the triple threat. In fact, we used to joke I was the quintuple threat – actor, singer, writer, magazine editor ... and insomniac. I moved here to find my big break – even if "working in theatre" ended up meaning ushering at the Adelphi. Well, that's not entirely true. Back in the day, I was part of most of the big musicals in the West End. Not the star of the show but always there in the ensemble.'

He swished his hands flamboyantly. 'Never mind all that. I can regale you with those stories another time. Steve told me he'd always had dogs but that his work had him travelling all over the world, so it wouldn't be fair to keep one now. He's originally from America, you know. But he's been based in London for the past decade or so.'

Madge's pen stopped for a moment and she looked up. 'What sort of work did he say he did?'

'He was in theatre. That's what we bonded over – a shared love of musical theatre. Well, of course, we both love all sorts of performance art. But musical theatre's our favourite.' He slapped his hand over his mouth. 'Would you listen to me – talking like there's still a *we* – still an *us*! As though there ever were.'

'I was a singer too.' Carole hauled the wheelie stool over and sat down facing Big Joe, an earnest look on her face. 'When I was nineteen, my boyfriend got me a gig singing at his nightclub. One day, he promised to introduce me to a well-known record producer – but it turned out it was a scam. I marched down to his club to tell that no-good bastard where he could shove his phoney record deal. Except when I got there, I saw him kill the sleazy producer. To escape his wrath, I went into hiding at a convent, where I taught the nuns to sing popular songs.'

Big Joe blinked. '*Sister Act* – that's the plot of *Sister Act*.'

Carole tapped the side of her head before standing up and walking to the window. Peggy looked at Big Joe and raised her hand, palm upwards.

'Ah.' Big Joe nodded slowly in response. 'Steve told me he was looking forward to settling down and finding some stability. He said he sometimes came to our dog park when he was in London – just to spend time with all the lovely dogs. Told me his favourite was an older shepherd who always wore a bright pink muzzle. That's Ozzy. I see him from my window sometimes. He doesn't care about dogs – all he wants is a bit of love from people. His human once told me he wears the muzzle to stop him eating everything in sight.'

Carole pressed her face to the window – though the Lord only knew why. Even Peggy couldn't always explain her partner's actions.

Big Joe spent a moment fussing Cookie before he continued. 'Anyhow, Steve said he wanted to settle down and buy a little place somewhere near here. He said we would get a little dog and he'd take her to the dog park every day. Steve was going to buy me a mobility scooter so I could join him on little adventures around the neighbourhood. There's a lovely little coffee shop on Tanner's Hill – he said I'd love it there. Do you know the place?'

The grin on Madge's face couldn't have been prouder. 'Wellbeloved. That's my daughter's café.' She gestured at her friends. 'Peggy and Carole and I are investors.'

A dainty little squeak erupted from Big Joe. 'You're them! You're the crafters!'

That stopped Peggy in her tracks. 'We what?'

Madge crossed her arms over her bosom. 'We are crafters – but what do you mean?'

'Steve told me there were four women who sat in the café and worked on their crafts. I was enamoured by the idea of these four women who got together every morning to knit, drink coffee, and have a bit of a natter. We were both so fascinated by you – we sometimes imagined what you got up to when you weren't in there drinking tea. And to think, now you're here, sitting in my parlour and drinking my tea!' He clapped like this was the most delightful thing he'd ever imagined.

Peggy's blood ran cold. She swapped glances with Madge and Baz. They all knew what this meant. Any lingering doubt that this scam was local in origin had just vanished in a puff of smoke.

Big Joe leant over the edge of his chair and pulled a computer onto his lap. 'Let me just find a text message where we talked about that – about you. I'm pretty sure I saved some screenshots. It's lucky, actually, because his profile's gone now. I think he's deleted all the messages he sent.'

He opened the device and spent a few moments clicking and swiping. 'Here. Come have a look.'

He turned the computer around to face Peggy and Madge. The two women leant forwards and peered at his screen.

'Actually... Now, don't look if you're prudish. Things get a wee bit not safe for work, if you get my drift.'

Peggy looked down at the screen. She'd seen worse. When she was a journalist, someone had once sent her notes alleged to have been written by a Tory government minister to a university student he was meant to be mentoring. A fair few of them alluded to 'that thing you did with the Rolodex'.

This had nothing on that.

'Ooh.' With her glasses on and her face screwed up, Madge waved a hand at the computer. '*That* sounds like fun.'

Baz stood up and walked over to get a peek. As her eyes scanned the screen, she turned a predictable shade of red – before the colour drained right out of her.

'Big Joe.' Baz swallowed. 'Do you have a photo of Steve – not just the little icon there but a bigger one?'

Big Joe turned the computer back around. 'Of course I do, love. But what's wrong, my dear? You look like you've swallowed a ghost.'

He was right. Baz appeared to be blinking back tears.

Big Joe clicked a few keys and then swung the computer around again so the women could get a look at the man on the screen. Steve was a middle-aged White man, unremarkable in every way. There was something familiar about him, but Peggy couldn't put her finger on it.

His appearance caused a strong reaction from Baz, though. She gasped and appeared to go weak in the knees. She moved back to her chair and dropped into it, weeping.

Carole wandered over to see what the fuss was about. She glanced at the computer screen. 'Aha!' She walked over to Baz and squeezed her shoulder. 'You made a ridiculous-looking man, Baz. Like they'd run you through the blue boringers. You're much better now. Much more yourself.'

Peggy looked at the screen and then at Baz and then at the screen. It felt like accidentally walking in on your friend naked. 'Close the computer, please, Big Joe.'

in which peggy receives an unexpected invitation

ON SUNDAY MORNINGS, Peggy and Carole always had a bit of a lie-in. It was the one day of the week Carole didn't start with a trip to the gym. They got up around ten and enjoyed a lazy morning.

Most Sundays, Peggy was happy for the break. While her lifestyle in retirement – such as it was – was hardly as frenetic as it had been back in her journalism days, her schedule was still fairly full. Between her activities with her friends, her writing, and making sure Cookie got sufficient exercise, her days were plenty busy. But she'd passed her next book off to her beta readers, so there wasn't much to do on that front.

Friday's incident with Baz's photo was still weighing on her mind. They'd spoken on Friday after leaving Big Joe's, of course. Baz had been shaken up about it. Peggy and Madge had both messaged Baz on Saturday to be sure she was all right. She insisted she was, but Peggy wasn't sure she believed her.

What did it all mean? It couldn't have been an accident. Why would someone dig up old photos of Baz and use them for nefarious purposes? It didn't make any sense!

And now they'd struck a bit of a dead end in their search for this fraudster.

They were certain it was all the handiwork of one person or group of people. They knew the pattern of how he approached his intended victims. They knew the name he'd been going by, though it was common enough that searches turned up nothing useful. Madge and Peggy had checked with the victims they were in contact with. Both Mitch and Suzy had confirmed the pre-transition photo of Baz was the man they knew as Stephen Wright.

They'd looked into the various account details the victims had been asked to deposit funds into. Three appeared to be prepaid credit cards. The Cash App, PayPal, and Revolut accounts had all been closed since the victims had figured out what he was up to.

With no further leads and no ideas for where to look next, Peggy was restless. She scratched her head, then studied her hands. She could repaint her fingernails. But the green polish was only a few days old and had barely started to chip.

She stood up from the sofa and paced around the living room for a few minutes – but Cookie thought it meant they were going for another walk. And her hip was giving her grief. Instead, she made her way to the bookshelf; she selected one she hadn't read in a while: *Second Shot* by Cindy Dees. A story about a semi-retired female assassin should help calm her nerves.

She settled back on the sofa next to Carole and opened the book. She stared at the first page for far longer than should have been necessary before conceding her mind wasn't in it right now.

Peggy was about to suggest they splurge on a roast dinner at one of the many local pubs when Carole's mobile rang out with the sounds of Rage Against the Machine's 'Killing in the Name'.

Carole pulled the device from her handbag and glanced at the screen before lifting it to her face with a broad grin. 'Morning, love. I've been meaning to tell you to watch your water supply. It's only safe to drink bottled. The taps these days run with the blood of wolves rounded up off the streets. And of course, we all know they're pumped full of—'

She paused while the person on the other end of the line spoke. Peggy could hear the voice but not the words. It sounded like one of the twins: Harvey Junior or Ronnie. Ronnie wasn't close to his family – metaphorically or geographically – so it was presumably Harvey Junior.

'All right, dear. See you then. Remind me to tell you all about the time I travelled home for my sister's funeral. I was starting to suspect that her death wasn't an accident and so I followed a complex web of lies and cover-ups through Nantwich's criminal underworld to find the woman who ordered my sister's death.'

Peggy had never been to Nantwich, a sleepy market town in Cheshire. And she wasn't sure Carole had either. She certainly wasn't from there and nor did she have a sister. But had she ever lived a gender-swapped *Get Carter*?

Who could say for certain with Carole?

'All right, love. I'll see you then. Do you need me to bring my rolling pin?' After a moment, Carole handed the phone to Peggy. 'He wants to talk to you.'

Peggy glanced at the screen before raising the phone to her ear. 'Harvey Junior.'

'Peggy.' His voice was as flat as his working-class south-east London accent would allow for. 'Just wanted to let you know Mum's agreed to come for dinner this evening.'

'I'll remind her. What time do you want her there?'

'No, sorry.' She envisioned him squeezing his eyes shut as he gripped his forehead between his thumb and forefinger. 'What I'm trying to say is I want for *both* of you to come, innit.'

'Oh?' Well, that was a surprise. It wasn't that she and Harvey Junior had anything against one another. Okay, maybe it was exactly that. He didn't like his mother being with a woman and she didn't care for the mindless violence of his life-style. Violence should be reserved for only the most worthy cases.

'Yeah, just...' He sounded as though he were speaking through gritted teeth. 'Just be here at seven ... if that's all right with you, of course. There's something I need to talk to you about – to both of you, I mean.'

Curious. 'All right. We'll be there.'

'Good,' he said.

'Fine.'

'I'll see you later, then.' He disconnected the call, leaving Peggy staring at the device, wondering what on earth she was in for.

When Peggy and Carole first got together, Carole's oldest three children were in their early twenties and had already moved out of the family home. Tina, the youngest, had been fifteen. She'd lived with the couple until she'd finished her master's degree in psychology. In fact, she'd moved back in again a year later when she decided she couldn't work in the field. She'd stayed with them while she studied creative writing, only moving out for good after she got the cheque for her first ghostwriting gig. Peggy's relationship with Tina was solid. She considered the young woman the daughter she'd never had.

Not that she'd ever had the slightest interest in having kids.

Still, if she had found herself in that situation somehow, she could do far worse than Tina.

On the few occasions she'd spent time around Ronnie, Peggy thought they got on all right.

But Peggy's relationship with Harvey Junior and Diane remained ... strained. Diane was the worst. She'd made it clear to all and sundry that she resented Peggy's presence in her mother's life. She'd been referring to Carole's relationship with Peggy as 'Mum's midlife crisis' for twenty years now. The fact that referring to someone who was sixty-six years old as being 'midlife' implied they would live to well past a hundred seemed entirely lost on Diane.

Diane still called Peggy her mother's *friend*. And Harvey Junior had always been inclined to take his sister's side in any argument. When Carole spent time with either of them ... Peggy wasn't invited.

So, to be asked to join them for dinner at Harvey Junior's home was ... unexpected. She thought he lived somewhere in Greenwich – quite local – but she didn't know exactly where.

This was going to be an interesting evening.

———

PEGGY STEERED her rickety older-model mobility scooter over the pedestrian bridge spanning Deptford Creek near of where it fed into the Thames. Carole wandered a bit ahead and Cookie walked neatly by Peggy's side.

Once they'd crossed the bridge, they paused by the railing to peer out across the river. This spot offered stunning views. Straight across was Canary Wharf. To the right, the little glass onion dome of the south end of the pedestrian tunnel was visible. To the left, they could see the Shard and bits of the City in the distance.

The sun wouldn't go down for a few hours yet, but it was

already somewhat low over the western sky, tinging everything a delicate pink. 'Such a beautiful day,' Peggy said.

She had to assume Carole knew where she was going. Which is to say, she *definitely* knew where they were going. Of course, that didn't rule out leading them on a wild goose chase all over south-east London, only to reveal Harvey Junior actually lived next door to them.

Peggy didn't think he lived that close, but it was something Carole would do.

After a few moments of admiring the view, Carole turned and set off again. She headed into the warren of buildings directly behind them. She walked to a door and pressed a buzzer. Instead of the responding voice Peggy expected, the unlock buzzer sounded. She looked closer and noticed a tiny camera embedded in the wall. Presumably the person on the other end of the buzzer wasn't simply granting entry to any random person who happened along.

They made their way through the building and into the lift. Carole walked as though she knew where she was going, so Peggy and Cookie trundled along in her wake.

They exited the lift on the building's top floor. No sooner had Carole turned right than a door was flung open and a giant of a man stepped into the tastefully decorated corridor and opened his arms. 'Mum!' Carole stepped up and allowed herself to be embraced by her mountain of a son.

'People keep coming around and asking me if I have kids.' Carole's voice was strained by the tight embrace of her son. 'I tell them I'm not a goatherd.'

Cookie ran to join the hug. Well, it would be more accurate to say he shambled over to them, but that was a run as far as Cookie was concerned.

The man gave Cookie a thorough cuddle before looking up. 'Peggy.' His words weren't cold – not exactly. But there was none of the warmth with which he'd addressed his mother. Or even Cookie.

'Come on in. You can leave the scooter out here. Dinner's almost ready.' He moved out of the way so they could all enter. Cookie headed into the flat without waiting. Carole paused to help Peggy up.

Peggy's eyes opened wide as she walked into the flat. What a space! The large open-plan living/dining room featured floor-to-ceiling windows. You could fit Carole and Peggy's whole two-bedroom flat into this one room. It was bigger and more luxurious even than Baz's flat. Everything was tastefully – and expensively – decorated in clichéd neutral tones. The furniture looked like it was designed for style rather than comfort. Several pieces of bland art on the wall were taller than Peggy.

But it was what lay beyond those remarkable windows that took Peggy's breath away. The view was the same as the one they'd just admired from the footpath. But from the tenth floor, they could see so much further. Absolutely stunning. And with the balcony doors open, the sound of the waves lapping on the shore filled the space. She couldn't help but let herself be drawn outside.

Even the word 'balcony' was misleading. The outdoor space was at least as big as the indoor space. A very solid-looking outdoor dining table had been set with three places.

'Best view in the world, innit?' Harvey Junior placed a glass of wine in Peggy's hand.

'Thank you.' She accepted the glass.

'It's a Turkish chardonnay.' He looked her in the eye and touched his glass to hers. 'One of my favourites. And very reasonably priced.'

Peggy lifted the glass to her lips, sniffing before she took a sip. 'Very nice. Refreshing. Thank you.'

Harvey inclined his head. 'I tried to get Tina to join us but she's still too upset about everything that's been going on.'

'Ah. She told you...' Peggy let her voice trail off. She wasn't sure what he knew. She didn't want to betray Tina's confidence.

'About this bloody scam?' He cocked an eyebrow. 'Too right she did. If I find the bastard, no one's going to have to worry about him anymore – I'll tell you that for free.'

Peggy had no doubt about that, so she simply nodded before taking another drink.

'I'd best get back to the kitchen. Bottle's on the table if you need a top-up. Dinner won't be long. Please make yourself at home.' He set his glass on the table before stepping back into the flat.

Peggy stood, leaning on the balcony railing, admiring the view. On the other side of the open doors, she could hear Carole regaling Harvey Junior with another of her fantastical tales. She was pretty sure this one was Carole's take on the plot of the film *The Fugitive*. The sounds and smells of cooking wafted out, contrasting beautifully with the sounds of the river ten storeys below. Casting a glance over her shoulder, she spied Cookie begging for scraps.

After no more than ten minutes, the happy threesome joined her on the terrace. Harvey Junior held three shallow bowls, and Carole carried three glasses as well as a second bottle of wine.

'Dinner's served,' announced Harvey Junior. 'Well, starter is, at any rate.' He laid a bowl at each place then motioned for the women to take their seats. 'Now, before I join you, is there anything else you think we might need?'

Carole selected a chair. 'The waste water from urban laundromats is fed into the domestic water supply.'

'Coming right up. Won't be a tick.' He turned and stepped back into the flat.

Peggy sat down next to Carole at the round dining table.

Harvey Junior returned a moment later with a carafe of water in one hand and three stacked lowball glasses in the other. 'Now, don't say I never did nothing for you, Mum.' He distributed the glasses before taking his own seat. 'This is a fig, spinach, and summer squash salad. Bon appétit!'

Peggy looked at her own plate for a moment before tucking in. It was a beautifully presented, brightly coloured dish. She helped herself to a mouthful, taking care to get a good mix of the various items. The flavour combination that flooded her senses was exquisite. 'That's divine. You're a very good cook.' She wasn't sure what else to say. This whole evening was awkward and a bit uncomfortable – but at least the food was good.

Harvey Junior swallowed his own mouthful then dabbed at his lips with the napkin that had been on his lap – a gesture so dainty it stood in stark contrast to his physical presence. 'Thank you.'

He took a sip of his wine and, from the look on his face, Peggy figured he was about to reveal the reason behind this awkward encounter.

Harvey Junior set the glass back on the table and slowly exhaled. 'An acquaintance of mine recently brought me' – he made a loose gesture with his hand – 'shall we say an *opportunity*?'

Peggy set her fork down and looked at him. 'Oh?' She wasn't sure what else she was meant to say.

He rested his elbows on the table and steepled his fingers in front of his face. 'Let's call it ... a unique business venture involving a facility that provides opportunities for individuals to engage in relationship-building services, leveraging their interpersonal skills in a way that enhances emotional connections.'

Peggy furrowed her brow, feeling completely lost.

'This initiative,' he continued, 'aims to create a supportive environment for personal interactions, fostering connections that can lead to mutually beneficial outcomes.'

'What's that when it's at home?' Peggy studied the younger man.

'Let's not dance around – you know what line of work I'm in.'

She crossed her arms over her chest. 'I'm led to believe it's violent thuggery.' She shouldn't antagonise him – she really shouldn't. But sometimes she just couldn't help herself.

'If that's the phrase you'd like to use. Though I'd prefer to call myself an entrepreneur with a diverse investment portfolio.' He cocked an eyebrow at her. 'Mind you... Your hands aren't so clean themselves, from what I understand.'

Peggy bobbed her head in acknowledgement. There was some truth to his words. She didn't know how much he knew – presumably not everything. 'I'm still not connecting the dots. You haven't explained what this "unique business venture" is nor what it has to do with why I'm here.'

Harvey Junior leant forwards. 'By my understanding, this venture is what some might call romance fraud. I gather the opportunity includes two contract workers and all the technical bits and bobs they might need in the course of their business dealings.'

Peggy's jaw was hanging somewhere around her clavicle. Her mother, were she present, would have stuffed something into her mouth and chided her for such an uncouth display.

'Cat got your tongue, I take it?' He took hold of the wine glass and rolled the stem between his thumb and forefinger. 'Now, bear in mind, this was brought to me by an intermediary – a broker of sorts. What I found most surprising was the name of the seller.'

Peggy and Harvey Junior remained in a sort of stalemate for several heartbeats while Carole dunked her figs in her wine and hummed to herself.

Ice water flowed through Peggy's veins. She couldn't say what she expected him to say, but she knew that whatever he said next would change the course of the investigation – and possibly her life.

'Who?' she breathed.

Harvey Junior lifted the glass to his lips and took an agonisingly slow breath before responding. 'It was you, Peggy.'

The bottom fell out of her world.

'You – and that new friend of yours. Beverley ... no. Barbara something, innit?'

CHAPTER 10

wherein baz should have known better

For Baz, Sundays were her days for doing household chores. Laundry, hoovering, watering the plants. Except she'd finished most of her tasks yesterday.

It's amazing how much work a person could accomplish when she was determined to avoid thinking about why a fraudster was using her wedding photo as bait.

Often, on Sundays, she'd take a bit of a break so she and Daisy could enjoy a vegan roast dinner at one of the many local pubs in Deptford or nearby Greenwich, New Cross, or Brockley.

As Baz enjoyed her morning coffee – still refusing to think about the photo she saw on Friday – Daisy walked into the living room, yawning and stretching. 'Ugh. Sorry. Excuse me. Morning, Nan.'

Baz made a show of looking at her watch. 'Oh, would you look at that – you're right. It *is* still morning.'

Daisy squinted at her phone. 'Only just. I didn't get home from work until almost three.' She yawned again.

Baz raised a hand to her mouth. 'Oh, don't do that. You'll

get me started.' She pulled herself to her feet. 'Let me make you a coffee.'

'Cheers.' Daisy climbed up onto one of the tall stools at the breakfast bar. 'Ugh. I'm struggling to brain this morning.'

Baz flipped the bean-to-cup espresso machine back on. 'You're not overdoing it – are you?'

Daisy dropped her face onto the counter and folded her hands over her head. 'No, not overall. Maybe last night, though. A few of us stayed after the pub had closed. We sat around chatting. Geoff's having boy trouble, so we were all trying to' – she sat up and waved her arms around formlessly – 'boost his spirits, I suppose.'

Baz waited until the coffee machine finished the noisiest part of its cycle before speaking. 'If you're too tired, we don't have to go for Sunday lunch.'

Daisy's eyes opened wide for the first time that morning. 'What? No! Of course I still want to go.'

Baz felt a small rush of relief flow through her as she set the cappuccino in front of the girl. 'I was thinking we could head into Greenwich and go to one of the riverside pubs. Unless you don't feel like walking that far?'

Daisy took a long drink of the coffee and sighed contentedly. 'Oh, that sounds perfect.' She spun around on her stool and looked at the glorious sunshine. 'We'd better see if we can make a reservation, though. I don't want to walk all that way only to find out everywhere's already booked up.'

She pulled her phone from the kangaroo pocket of her hoodie and began clicking and swiping. 'The Old Brewery at one?'

Baz switched the coffee machine off and put the oat milk back in the fridge. 'Works for me. Can they fit us in?'

There was a glint in Daisy's eye as she looked up. 'Will the handsome Paul be joining us?'

Baz frowned. 'I asked him about it a few days ago but he dodged the question. I think he might be running cold on me.'

'Oh no, Nan.' Daisy's shoulders fell. 'I'm sorry. What makes you say that?'

Baz wiped the countertop down before making her way back to the lounge end of the room and settling into the sofa. 'Every time I suggest going out anywhere, he declines. He seems happy enough to cook for me at his place or here – but he demurs whenever talk turns to going out.' She twisted the chiffon of her skirt in her fingers. 'I think maybe he's embarrassed to be seen with me.'

Everything was unravelling around her. It was hard enough trying to figure out her relationships with Hari and Paul – she didn't have the emotional bandwidth to think about that bloody photo.

Daisy got up and strode across the room. She took the seat next to her grandmother before leaning forwards and setting her coffee mug on a coaster on the table. 'First of all, if anyone ever says or even implies that, then that person does not deserve your time.'

Baz smiled and patted the girl's arm. 'Thank you—'

'Second of all.' Daisy cut Baz off with an index finger. 'No way. That's not—'

'Oh, come on.' Baz shook her head. 'Look at me! I'm not—'

'Don't.' Daisy turned on the sofa so she was looking Baz full in the face. She folded her legs up under herself in a way Baz hadn't been able to do in decades. 'Just don't. I know there are people out there who'll judge us as soon as they see us. Or even without seeing us. But I'm not talking about *those* people – because they don't matter. I'm talking about you and Paul. And I guarantee' – Daisy made little circles with her fingers to emphasise her point – 'that that man is proud to be seen with you. That weird, camp, dapper little man wants nothing more than to be seen with you.'

Baz frowned. 'Then why doesn't he want to come out with us for lunch? Or dinner? Or drinks?'

Daisy screwed her face up. 'Have you two had the talk yet?'

'Of course he knows I'm trans!' said Baz. 'He is—'

'I know.' Daisy waved her hand playfully at Baz. 'That's not what I meant, silly. I'm talking about the *money* talk.'

Baz's mouth fell open.

Daisy put her hand on her grandmother's knee. 'You're in a mixed-wealth relationship. You know that, right?'

'What?'

Daisy waved a hand around herself, indicating the flat. 'You are wealthy, Nan. Paul's in his sixties and he works a minimum-wage job. He lives in a council flat that he shares with two randos.'

Baz blinked. 'What?'

'Oh, come on.' Daisy picked her mug back up and drained the last of it in one swallow. 'You *have* to know what that implies.'

Heat warmed Baz's cheeks. 'I guess I just never thought of it that way.'

'Well, you should think of it.' Daisy slapped her knees and stood up. 'Right. Guess I better get ready if we're going to make it to Greenwich for one.'

Baz was left on her own to consider that she might be the one in the wrong. How could she have missed that? And why was the scammer using her photo?

———

HALF AN HOUR LATER, Daisy held the building's main door

open as Baz steered her mobility scooter out onto the fore-court. The pair turned left and headed for the main road.

As they waited for the light to change so they could cross, Daisy turned to Baz with a certain cheeky sparkle in her eye. 'So?'

Baz swallowed. 'What?'

'You going to tell me what's going on with Baba?' Daisy nudged Baz with her elbow.

Baz kept her eyes fixed on the pedestrian walk light, willing it to change. 'I'm not sure what you mean?' She also wasn't sure why that came out as a question.

Daisy wagged her finger. 'Don't give me that. You think I don't know my own grandfather's voice? You've been talking to Baba lately. I've heard his voice coming out of your room at least three times now.'

At long last, the walk light appeared. Baz gripped her accel-erator and shot away from the pavement faster than intended.

'Okay, okay.' Even Daisy's long legs were struggling to keep up with the scooter's top speed. 'You don't have to tell me anything you don't want to. I was only teasing.'

'Sorry, love.' Baz cranked the knob to lower the speed to a pace Daisy could more easily match. 'Yes, Hari and I have been talking lately. It's been...' She pinched her lips together, uncer-tain where that sentence was heading.

Daisy smiled. 'I'm sorry, Nan. It must be tough. You two were so close for so long. Starting over has got to be difficult.'

Baz spent a few moments trying to gather her thoughts before responding. 'Talking to Hari... In some ways, it feels like coming home. I've been catching him up on all the goings-on in our community.' Not *all* the goings-on, obviously. But she'd told him about her new friends and about the neighbourhood.

'Baba's from Southgate, right?' Daisy asked as they passed the Premier Inn on Greenwich High Road.

'Southall,' Baz replied. Like her, Hari had been born in London. His family had moved to Canada at a similar time to Baz's. It was one of many things they had bonded over.

'And that's not south, is it?'

Baz chuckled. 'No. It's way out west. Near Heathrow. His mum's thinking of moving back – did you know that?' She shook her head. 'She's eighty years old! I can't even imagine moving halfway round the world at her age.'

Daisy poked her in the shoulder. '*You* moved halfway round the world a year ago!'

'Excuse me!' Baz felt a sharp jolt when she accidentally released the accelerator. 'I'm in my sixties – it's hardly the same thing.'

With a small laugh, Daisy said, 'All right. Fair enough. What are you going to do about Baba, then? Are you two getting back together?'

'No! I mean, yes. I have no idea.' Baz frowned. 'I don't even know what I want.'

'And that's perfectly okay,' Daisy replied.

They passed by Greenwich train station on their left. Baz remembered when she used to walk distances like this without needing to rely on the scooter. Those days were in her past now. But still, the scooter gave her a chance at freedom.

'But don't leave Paul hanging on for too long, eh?'

Baz glanced up at Daisy for a second, before returning her focus to where she was going. 'Sorry, dear. What?'

'Paul?' Daisy sighed. 'It's okay that you need some time to figure out what you want. Really, it is. But don't keep Paul hanging on. That sweet, lovely man deserves better.'

Baz winced inwardly. 'I'm not leading him on. I'm not. Well, I'm not trying to. It's just...' Her voice trailed off – she couldn't figure out what she was trying to say.

'Complicated?'

Baz bobbed her head in assent. 'It is. Paul is wonderful. Being with him is ... he gets it. You know? He sees me for who I am and he likes me anyways. He never knew me as ... well, before. And he knows what it's like.'

'I get that.' Daisy pressed the button on the walk light, waiting to cross Creek Road.

'But with Hari, there's so much history.' Baz steered her scooter out into the road when the light changed. 'He's known me for forty years – that's almost two-thirds of my life. And I know him. It's familiar and comfortable.'

As Baz parked outside the pub, Daisy screwed up her face. 'It's just...' She held her hand out to help Baz out of the scooter. 'Don't let him hurt you. Not again.'

'No.' Baz frowned as they walked to the door of the pub. 'He was very supportive of my transition, you know.'

'But...' Daisy dragged the word out. 'He also rejected you because of it. And that's not cool.'

A host took their names and directed them to a table out on the patio. The pub wasn't quite close enough to see the water, though the Thames was only about twenty-five metres away. Their table faced the *Cutty Sark*, the world-famous ship. It was now situated next to the river and had been converted to a museum.

Once they were seated and the host had left them, Baz studied her fingernails. She really needed to go for another manicure. 'Daisy.'

Daisy looked up from the menu she was studying. 'Yeah?'

'You know it's not Hari's fault that he didn't want to be with a woman, right?'

Daisy gave a melodramatic sigh and then stared at her grandmother. 'He *was* with a woman!' Baz opened her mouth to respond but Daisy wasn't finished. 'For forty years!'

'Thirty,' Baz said, before waving a hand. 'And not really.'

Daisy crossed her arms over her chest and raised her eyebrows.

Baz sighed. 'I mean, yes. I am a woman. I've always been a woman. But I hadn't acknowledged it when I got together with Hari. I don't think I knew who I was back then. So you can't blame him for—'

'BS!'

Baz leant back in her chair. 'Daisy, where has this come from? I thought you loved Hari? You've always had such a good relationship with him.'

Daisy shrugged. 'I do. And I do. But I can also see how much his rejection hurt you.'

'He didn't reject—'

'He *did*.' Daisy crossed her arms again. 'He was supportive blah blah blah. But you were still the same person. Don't you see that? All you did was acknowledge that. You didn't change yourself – you became *more* yourself.'

'Yes, and he—'

Daisy wagged her finger. 'No. Don't give me that. He's a good person but he did a bad thing. And because of that, he'll never have my full trust again. I respect him and I'm not saying I don't trust him at all. I do – you know I do. But I'm also a bit wary around him now.'

Baz's mouth was dry. 'That's not fair.'

Daisy tapped a sky-blue fingernail against the menu. 'Do you know what you want to order?'

Allowing her granddaughter to change the subject, Baz told her what she wanted. Daisy excused herself to go to the bar, leaving Baz alone with her thoughts. Thoughts of anything but her relationships. Or that terrible photo.

in which dinner is served

PEGGY SWALLOWED as her insides turned to liquid. She had expected this evening to be awkward. She'd anticipated slinging verbal arrows with Carole's erudite yet brutish son. She had known full well he'd invited her for a reason. While she hadn't known what that reason might be, never in a million years would she have expected him to accuse her of being behind the romance fraud plaguing the residents of south-east London.

This twelfth-floor balcony no longer seemed like a stylish urban retreat; now, it was a death trap.

Tina – Carole's daughter and Harvey Junior's sister – had been a victim of this fraudster. There wasn't anything Harvey Junior wouldn't do to protect his family. In fact, Peggy harboured a secret theory about how and why Harvey Senior had met his untimely end.

She and Carole had never discussed the circumstances around his death. But the idea that an experienced sailor would suddenly decide to take his boat out while drunk never sat right with her. Peggy had assumed from the start that Harvey Junior was somehow behind his father's death. If he was, then –

given how protective he was of his mother – Peggy figured it must have been done in defence of Carole.

Whether he killed his father or not, Peggy knew for certain that he had people on hand to dispose of inconvenient dead bodies or to tidy up crime scenes. She and her friends had made use of his connections on occasion themselves.

And now, here she was, in the home of a stone-cold killer. And he thought she'd hurt his sister. Her heart was beating like a racehorse – in fact, her insides hammered like Ascot on race day. Could she get out of the flat before he caught her? Carole and Cookie were safe with him; there was no doubt of that. Alas, she was almost twice his age and her hips were crumbling and useless.

Would Carole save her? Against anyone else in the world, the answer was a resounding yes. She'd demonstrated that multiple times. But against Harvey Junior? Peggy wasn't so sure.

For his part, Cookie may look fearsome but on the two occasions Peggy had been threatened – nothing serious but the point still stands – he'd done his very best imitation of a drooling statue.

'I...' Her mouth turned to sand. All the liquid in her had relocated to her guts. 'Har—'

Harvey Junior reached out but stopped short of touching her. 'Now listen, Peg.'

No one called her Peg. Not ever. But she wasn't about to interrupt him when he held his life in her hands.

'I know it ain't you.' He didn't withdraw his hand but turned it palm outwards. 'And I assume you'll vouch for this Bev, am I right?'

'Baz.' Peggy felt like a balloon cut loose.

His brow furrowed – confused. 'What?'

Peggy swallowed. 'Her name is Barbara. She goes by Baz.'

He shrugged. 'Whatever. My point is that you trust her, yeah?'

'One hundred per cent,' Peggy said. 'I trust her with my life.' She wagged her finger. 'Back up just a moment. What do you mean you know it wasn't me? You hate me.'

Harvey Junior's eyebrows lifted ever so slightly. 'You're the one who hates me.'

'What?'

'You've always refused to join Mum when she comes for family dinners.' He picked up his fork and speared a spinach leaf and a chunk of squash.

'Refused?' Peggy ran a hand through her spiky hair. 'You don't invite me. You make a point of not inviting me.'

He swallowed his mouthful and dabbed at his lips with his napkin. 'Well, I don't anymore. For years, we'd get the whole clan together for Sunday dinners. Back before Ronnie moved to Germany. I think you joined us once.'

'Twice.'

He lifted a hand. 'Oh, that's right. Christmas of 2007. The one where—'

'Quite.' Peggy frowned.

He chuckled. '*That's* all it took to scare you away? I thought you were stronger than that.'

Peggy inhaled through her nose. 'I am very strong – thank you. But I know when I'm not wanted. Why should I subject myself to a room full of people who hate me?'

'That's just Diane.' Harvey Junior waved her words away. 'Diane hates everyone.'

Peggy scoffed. 'She's certainly the leader of the pack.'

Now it was Harvey Junior's turn to scoff. 'You think because we ignore her, that makes her our leader? You posh twats have a strange view of leadership.'

'I am not a posh twat.' Peggy set her loaded fork back down

and considered. 'Well, not anymore.' She shrugged. 'That is, I try not to be.'

The conversation fell into a brief lull as they finished the last morsels of their salads in tense, loaded silence.

Harvey laid his fork down across his plate. 'So, let me get this straight. The reason you stopped coming to family dinners is because Diane was mean to you? I really thought you was better than that.'

Peggy drained the rest of her wine in one go. 'No, the reason I stopped coming to family dinners is because no one seemed to mind Diane being cruel to me. I was under the impression you all felt the same. Well, except Carole and Tina, obviously.'

He nodded. 'You done a world of good for that kid. She was adrift after our dad ... well, you know. You were a better father to her than he ever was.' He shrugged. 'I suppose that's not very politically correct. You know, what with you being a woman and all. But you know what I mean.'

Peggy bit back a chuckle. 'Gender schmender. But thank you. That's kind ... in a way. I didn't know you felt that way.'

Harvey Junior held his hands out, palms up. 'Yeah, well, you never got to know me. Did you?' He slid his chair back from the table and stood up. 'Come help me with the main. Er, would you mind?'

'Not at all.' Peggy smiled gratefully. 'Of course.'

Harvey Junior looked at Carole. 'You all right, Mum? Anything you need while we're up?'

Carole smiled sweetly as she clasped his hands. 'Of course, the Etruscans had such different theories from the Patagonians regarding the nature of the universe. You know that, don't you?'

He returned her grin as she patted his cheek. 'Of course. Coming right up.'

Peggy followed him into the kitchen. He pulled a large pan

from the hanging rack and set it in the sink. A special tap off to the side dispensed steaming water. Once he was satisfied with the volume, he set the pan on the hob and flicked a switch. Flames leapt into life beneath the pan. Harvey Junior opened the fridge and removed a tray. 'Smoky aubergine ravioli. Made them fresh this afternoon.'

'You made the ravioli?' Peggy was starting to see there was more to this man than met the eye.

'Seems there's a lot we don't know about each other.' He carefully floated each parcel in the boiling water before turning his attention to a smaller pan on the hob.'So, if you're not behind this little scheme and you trust this—' He waved a hand.

When he lifted the lid, Peggy's nostrils were flooded with the scents of roasted tomatoes and garlic and assorted herbs. 'Baz,' she supplied.

'Thank you. If you trust that Baz isn't the one behind it, then the question we need to ask ourselves is—'

'Who's setting us up?' Peggy furrowed her brows.

'Exactly.' It wasn't long before he began plating up the ravioli, taking care with his presentation. He drizzled the creamy tomato sauce over the top before turning back to the fridge. He returned to the plates a moment later with a plastic carton. 'A little dash of micro greens makes the whole thing so much more visually appealing – don't you think?'

Peggy's mouth was watering, even as her brain was racing to catch up. She turned to see Cookie next to her, leaving a little pool of drool on the floor in front of himself. 'I can't blame you, mate.'

'What was that?'

'Someone's excited about your food.' She indicated Cookie. 'And I must say, it smells incredible.'

'I suppose that's one of those things you didn't know about me – am I right?'

Peggy conceded it was.

'Now don't get me wrong. I know I have a certain ... reputation.' He collected the three plates. 'There's a bottle of red there next to the fridge – would you mind grabbing that?'

Peggy plucked the wine – a Serbian merlot – from its resting place and followed him across the large room.

'My work isn't always above board.' He paused at the balcony door and took care as he stepped over the lip. 'And you're right. Sometimes I need to employ certain – shall we say – enhanced persuasion techniques. You can decide for yourself whether that makes me a—' He set a plate down in front of his mother. 'Here you go, Mum.' The next plate went to Peggy's spot. Lastly, he set the third plate in front of his own chair and then accepted the bottle from Peggy.

The red wine glasses were already on the table. He took the one from in front of Carole. 'May I?'

'King James the First worked with Cleopatra to write the computing language,' she said.

He handed her the glass with a small amount of liquid.

'Margaret Thatcher tried to stop them, of course. But we gave her what for.' She sniffed the wine and then tasted it. 'Mmm, I'm getting plum and cherry with a hint of motor oil. Just leave the bottle, would you?'

He handed her the bottle and passed her the other two glasses.

As Carole poured three generous glasses of wine, her son continued. 'As I was saying, you can decide for yourself whether that makes me a – what did you call me? Oh, yes. A violent thug. It's not an appellation I'd claim for myself but I can see why some might apply it to me.'

Peggy bobbed her head.

'But' – he extended his index finger – 'I won't have you thinking I'm some sort of homophobe. I don't abide hatred of people based on who they are. If I'm going to hate a person – and, trust me, there are plenty of people on this earth I hate – it's going to be for what they've done. Never for who they are. If we're going to be brutally honest here... The people I hurt – just like the people you hurt – they're bad people. Know what I'm saying?'

Peggy had to concede his point.

'I ain't never hated you.' Harvey Junior picked up his fork and knife and sliced open one of the pasta parcels. 'We ought to eat this before it gets cold.' He placed his loaded fork in his mouth and savoured his creation. 'Mmm. Oh, those turned out nicely.'

Peggy followed his lead with the food. It was indeed delicious. She very much doubted he was out there working to defend people from those who would prey on them. Perhaps he sometimes acted out of vengeance, but it would be personal vengeance, not protecting the community as a whole. But he had a point. Perhaps. 'I appreciate you saying that, Harvey Junior. And you should know I don't hate you – or any of your family.'

He raised his wine glass to his lips. 'Maybe Diane.' He held the thumb and index finger of his free hand close together. 'Just a bit?'

Peggy took a sip of her own wine. It was a perfect pairing. 'Diane is, from what I understand, every inch her father's daughter.'

He released a sort of half chuckle. 'Yeah, she is that. Our dad was ... complicated. Loving and loyal but also brutal and uncompromising. He had some pretty clear ideas about how the world worked – or at least how he thought it ought to.'

He swallowed another mouthful of the ravioli in its

exquisite sauce. 'And Diane believes all that same ... garbage. She thinks Muslims are invading and drag queens are corrupting the children. She says Poles are somehow both benefits scroungers and stealing all our jobs. It's more than enough hate for one family. There's no point arguing with her – believe me, I've tried.'

Peggy thought of her own family. Most of them believed the same things – yet she knew down to the tips of her toes that they'd look down on Diane for being inferior.

Harvey Junior drained his wine glass and set it back on the table. 'Diane's family. She's my sister and I love her. But that don't mean I agree with her. I know words ain't gonna change her mind – certainly not coming from me. Look, she's an idiot. I know that. But this ain't about her – it's about me and you. I don't hate you, Peggy. You been good for Mum. And good for Tina. I'm glad Mum's got you in her life.'

Carole polished off her wine and stood up. She began waltzing around the terrace – her arms wrapped around an imaginary dance partner – singing Monty Python's 'Always Look on the Bright Side of Life'.

Peggy smiled at her partner before dragging her eyes back to Carole's son. 'Thank you, Harvey Junior. I appreciate that. And for my part, I'm sorry I made assumptions.'

She paused as he refilled her wine glass. 'Now, about this business venture. Who told you Baz and I were the sellers?'

He chewed his lips, looking like he was weighing up how much to reveal. 'Obviously, Tina was targeted by ... someone like that. You could say my hackles was up. So I asked one of my guys to do a bit of digging. I'm not going to talk about who they are or how they found the information. My business wouldn't be successful if I went around blabbing all my secrets.'

'All right.' Peggy considered that for a moment. 'I don't need – or, quite frankly, want – all your secrets. But we need something to go on. If we want to get ... justice for what was done to Tina and for all the other victims we've met, then we need some kind of clue as to where to look next. Who we should talk to. We've spoken to five people who've been swindled by him. The amounts we're talking about may not seem like big money to you – but for several of the victims, we're talking about their life savings.'

Carole was still dancing. The song she was singing revolved around a person encountering his own penis on display at a car boot sale.

Peggy crossed her arms over her small chest. 'We need to prevent this miscreant from causing any more pain. I won't let him hurt anyone else. He needs to be ... stopped. Once and for all.' She knew he understood her quite plainly. 'Please, Harvey Junior. Give us something to work with.'

His face went stony and the silence dragged out. 'This opportunity was brought to me by a colleague. Someone who has earned my trust. After my investigation, I pressed my associate for some additional information. They told me the deal had come to them from... Well, I suppose you could call them a broker of sorts.'

'Okay.'

Harvey Junior slid his chair back from the table. 'Come on. Let's get dessert and I'll put some coffee on.'

Peggy stood up. She noticed a serving tray leaning against the door, so she fetched it and added the empty wine glasses to it as Harvey Junior stacked the empty plates.

She and Cookie followed him back into the flat.

He took the tray from her and set it on the counter. 'It's a decaf espresso for you, right?' When she nodded, he opened up a cupboard that revealed a hidden coffee station, complete with high-end espresso machine. 'I managed to get the name of the broker but I need you to understand my name can't come into this. A lot of strings were pulled and favours called in to get this information – you get me?'

'I understand. We're the soul of discretion.'

Having weighed out the beans, he ran them through a single-dose grinder. When it finished, he leant back against the counter. 'All right. It's a guy called Mitch. I can get you his contact details.'

wherein a very brief tea party is held

THE NEXT DAY, the women had a very tense session at the café, in which time dragged. Afterwards, they all met up again at Baz's for lunch.

Once they'd loaded the dishes into the dishwasher and set it off, the women got ready to head out on their mission.

As Baz put her shoes on, Daisy regaled Peggy with her plans for Cookie. The dog suffered from severe separation anxiety and couldn't be left alone. And besides, the girl absolutely adored him. 'I still can't get over how much he looks like Sophie.'

On Sunday evening, Hari had sent Baz some recent pics of Sophie, their German shepherd, at a local dog park. Without noticing the name at the top of the message, she'd thought she was looking at Cookie. 'Spitting image.'

'You're just lucky I'm not working Mondays. Did Gran tell you I got *two* summer jobs? I'm working at one of the pubs on Deptford High Street and three days a week at a design firm in Southwark.'

'Well done, you.' Peggy took Cookie's face in her hands and gave him a quick snuggle. 'Now you be good for Daisy.'

'We shouldn't be more than an hour.' Baz took her handbag down from its hook on the wall and set it in the basket of her scooter.

'Maybe two,' said Madge.

'I've brought my special knitting needles.' Carole began rummaging in her bag. 'Would you like to see them?'

Peggy took her partner by the elbow and steered her out of the room. 'The girl's not interested in your ... crafting, my love.'

'Bye. And thank you,' Baz called as she closed the door.

They didn't have long to wait for the lift. As they travelled down the nine floors, Baz asked, 'Are we certain he's going to be home?'

Madge raised the nurse's watch she habitually wore and looked at the face. 'I spoke with his neighbour this morning. Mary's a lovely woman. She had a hip replacement a few years ago after a bad fall.'

Peggy shook her head as the four of them exited the lift into the lobby. 'We're not interested in Mitch's neighbour's medical history, Madge. We only want to know how certain you are that the man himself is likely to be in.' She retrieved her own scooter – a smaller model than the one Baz rode – and took her seat.

Madge kissed her teeth. 'I was getting there. Yes, Mary assures me, he's typically in on Monday afternoons. He has a standing engagement on Monday evenings but he doesn't leave until gone five.'

After greeting the concierge on duty, Baz left the building with the others following close behind. She turned right instead of her normal left.

She steered her scooter around the outer edge of the building and then into the park.

The last time the women made this journey, they'd followed Brookmill Road – a busy urban thoroughfare. Today, they made their way through Brookmill Park, which ran parallel with the road but was separated from it by trees and a wall.

'I do love this park,' said Baz as she steered her scooter down the lush, verdant path that followed the River Ravensbourne. 'The scents, sights, and sounds of rural England – right in the heart of London.'

Peggy gestured with her left hand – keeping her right on her scooter's accelerator. 'I like watching the egrets.'

Baz looked where she was indicating and saw three of the large birds – two perched in a tree and a third standing on the riverbank. The one on the ground lifted and flew off into the trees. To their right, a couple of anglers sat on folding chairs.

'They don't allow dogs in the park,' Peggy added. 'Otherwise I'd come more often.'

At the end of the park, they bade farewell to Peggy and Carole. The pair would sit on a park bench and wait for Baz and Madge to return. If they weren't back in an hour, the other two would come to their rescue.

When the two women exited the park onto the road right in front of the nature reserve, Baz swallowed a lump in her throat. Six months ago, they had deposited the body of a serial killer in that very spot.

But that wasn't their destination today. They crossed the road and made their way to the next turning. Mitch's place was about halfway down the short street. Baz parked her scooter on the pavement in front of the house.

The pair approached the front door of an unassuming Victorian terraced house. Madge pressed the bell. This was immediately followed by a frantic, high-pitched barking.

Uneven footsteps could be heard on the other side of the door and a man's voice muttered, 'I'm coming – keep yer hair on.' When the door swung open, Mitch stood inside, cradling a small, white fluffy dog in the crook of his left elbow. He wasn't using crutches but he still had his right foot in the walking boot. 'Ladies. This feels familiar. I'm hoping you've come for more cordial purposes this time.' He peered around them. 'Where's your friends?'

His manner wasn't hostile but nor was it welcoming. Cautious, that was the word for it. Or perhaps Baz was projecting her own emotions onto him.

The women had discussed their intended approach over tea this morning and agreed they should try to keep this meeting cordial – hence the reduction in their number.

'It's just Barbara and I today.' Madge stood up to her full five foot four. 'May we come in?'

The mole below his right ear stretched as he smiled. 'Of course. So long as you're not here to try to persuade me to part with any more money, then I'm happy to let bygones be bygones.'

'We're not after any of your assets, I promise,' said Baz.

'And we've brought cakes.' Madge raised the bag containing the handmade goodies.

'All right.' He stepped aside to let them through, before bending to set the small dog down. 'Watch out for Truffles – he gets underfoot.' He grunted as he stood back upright, bracing himself on the wall.

Both women paused to remove their shoes before he ushered them past the tastefully appointed living room with its pale blue velvet suite. The long, narrow hallway led to an open-plan kitchen/dining area at the back of the property.

The large kitchen was modern and well appointed, as was the adjoining dining space. Everything was understated and top of the line. The far wall was filled with one of those bespoke sliding doors – the entire back wall was glass. 'I take it you've got something you'd like to discuss. Shall I put the kettle on?'

He was being far friendlier than he had the last time they'd visited. Baz wasn't quite sure what to make of it. She hoped his change of heart was sincere.

'Yes, please.' Madge set the bag of goodies on the counter. 'Where would I find plates and cutlery?'

As Mitch filled the kettle, he used his free hand to wave at a cupboard to his left. 'Just there.' He put the kettle on to boil and took a teapot and milk jug from a different cupboard.

Truffles was fussing at Baz's feet, so she bent down to pat the dog. 'You're a good little lad – aren't you?'

When she stood back up, Madge handed her a stack of small plates and a handful of cutlery. 'Take that through to the sitting room, would you?'

Mitch lifted the teapot and waved towards the back of the house. 'Why don't we head out to the garden instead?' He limped to the patio door and opened it one-handedly. The whole thing folded out of the way like an accordion. Truffles bolted past him and scampered about. 'Make yourselves at home. I'll be back in a mo with milk and sugar.' He set the teapot on the table before turning to head back into the house.

Baz couldn't imagine any world in which her friends would embrace Mitch – nor one where he'd even want to be one of them. And yet, he was behaving as though they were the best of friends. She knew in her heart of hearts that people could change. But was that what was happening here?

She put her bundle on the table and took a seat. Truffles immediately bounded over and sat down next to her, leaning into her ankles.

Madge set the cakes down and joined her.

The space was like a little urban oasis. The house shaded them from the early afternoon sun, but the small garden was lush and green. Everything smelled fresh and alive – lavender and rosemary and scents Baz couldn't identify.

She missed her garden back home in Edmonton. Mind you, Hari was the one with a green thumb. He'd fenced half their substantial garden off to grow fruit and veg. And he'd filled the front garden with roses and tulips and peonies and assorted other colourful flowers and plants. The whole place looked and smelled wonderful.

Baz returned to the here and now as Mitch took his seat. After pouring three cups of tea, he slid one to each of them. 'Now, as lovely as it is to see you both, let's cut to the chase. I want to know why you're here. When we spoke a few days ago, I got the sense you had everything you needed.' He leant back in his chair and waited for a response.

It took Baz a moment to realise what he was referring to. Mitch was one of the victims too – wasn't he? As she reached for the milk jug, she remembered she hadn't thought to ask if he had any oat milk. She didn't often put cow's milk in her tea – these days, the idea of it seemed strange to her. Still, drinking tea black was an even weirder idea, so needs must. She picked up the jug. As she poured it into her cup, she caught a whiff of something unexpected.

Mitch waved a hand. 'Sorry. That's coconut. Hope you don't mind – lactose intolerant, you know.'

Baz nodded then offered the jug to Madge, who added some to her own tea.

'We're here on an unusual mission.' Madge served up three slices of lemon cake and passed them around.

'Thank you.' Mitch accepted the proffered cake then waited for them to continue.

A squeak made Baz look down. She bit her lip to keep from chuckling at the sight of Truffles poised on his hind quarters with his front paws up in a pleading gesture. Clearly, he expected a bit of cake too.

Madge used her fork to slice off a sliver of cake. 'As you know, we've been looking into the romance fraud that's been targeting people in our community. I spoke to you earlier in the week as we discovered you were one of the people who'd been victimised.'

He swallowed a bit of cake. 'By Steve. That's right. I tell you – if I get my hands on him, I'd punch him right in the throat. No court would hold me liable – I promise you that.'

Madge took her little notebook from her pocket and set it on the table. 'Your name has come up a second time in our investigations.'

His eyebrows lifted ever so slightly. 'It has? How so?'

Madge and Baz looked at one another.

Baz set her mug on the table. 'It has been brought to our attention that you sometimes act as a broker of sorts.'

The smile that flashed across Mitch's face was so swift, she almost thought she imagined it. His cordiality with them seemed genuine – but something about that instant reaction struck Baz.

'Are you sure you don't have me confused with someone else?' He raised his tea to his mouth and took a long, slow drink.

'Now, see, that's what I thought at first.' Madge waved a hand at Baz. 'Didn't I say so? Mitch is a fairly common name, I said. But the details lined up too neatly.'

Baz nodded. 'We're not police – we don't care about your connections—'

Mitch barked a laugh. 'Funny. I could've sworn our last meeting suggested something quite different.'

Baz bit her lip. He was right. Of course he was.

But he waved her unspoken words away. 'No, no worries.

I'm only kidding. Or *mostly* kidding. Only I take pains to make sure very few people know about that part of my life. Suggests someone's been talking – someone who should know better.'

He set his mug down and studied each of them in turn. 'Though if anyone knows how persuasive you ladies can be, it's me. I've learnt my lesson. I won't be using *that* financial advisor again.' He patted his legs twice and Truffles leapt neatly into his lap. Mitch offered him a tiny morsel of cake. 'So, someone told you that I sometimes help facilitate certain business transactions between parties who wish to maintain a degree of ... shall we say anonymity. You looking to buy or to sell?'

'I think you misunderstand.' Madge wrapped her hands around her mug.

Mitch looked up. 'Oh?' Truffles, unimpressed with his master's shifting attention, pawed at his hand. He resumed fussing the dog.

'We're not looking to buy or to sell.' Madge ran a hand over her elaborate braids. She opened her notebook, then licked her finger and used it to flick through the pages.

Baz leant forwards in her seat. 'We're here because we want to talk about an opportunity you've been shopping around. We need to know who the seller is, as it concerns us directly.'

She couldn't see his face – Truffles was in the way. But when Mitch looked up, his face was calm, placid. 'Which opportunity are we talking about, then?' Truffles leapt off his lap circled the table.

'It concerns a local business that's up for sale.' Baz smiled at Truffles, who was pawing at her legs as though he wanted to be picked up. She patted her knees the way she'd seen Mitch do and the dog bounced energetically into her lap. He weighed absolutely nothing. For someone who'd been used to a thirty-five-kilogram dog, this little thing felt like no more than a bit of fluff. She let her hands sink into his silky white fur.

Mitch finished the rest of his tea and placed the mug back on the table. 'I'm afraid you're going to need to be a bit more specific than that.'

'Let me see.' Madge lifted her glasses – which hung on a chain around her neck – into place. She ran down the page of her notebook until she found the bit she was looking for. 'It was described to us as...' She tapped the page and looked Mitch in the eye before looking back to the book. 'We were told it was "an initiative aimed at creating a supportive environment for personal interactions, fostering connections that can lead to mutually beneficial outcomes."'

Mitch shrugged.

'It's romance fraud.' Baz stroked the dog's soft fur.

Mitch blinked. 'It's what?'

Madge's eyes opened wide. She tilted her head, looking over her glasses at him. 'It's like Baz says. This business opportunity you're selling—'

'*I* am not selling anything.' Mitch waved a finger. 'It's not mine to sell. My role is merely to facilitate. I'm a go-between. When buyers and sellers want to maintain an arm's length between themselves and their transactions.'

'Be that as it may.' Madge took her glasses off and let them hang from the chain.

Baz made to pick up her tea, but the dog tried to nose it out of her hands. 'This business that you're helping ... expedite the sale of. It's the very one that's been defrauding local residents.' She gave up trying to get to her tea and scratched the dog's ears instead. 'Including you.'

Madge fixed him with a piercing stare. 'You're helping *facilitate* your own victimisation.'

Mitch nodded slowly. 'I wasn't aware of that.' He looked off into the greenery over the back fence, chewing his cake in silence.

The instant Baz set her fork down on her plate, he pushed his chair back and stood up, the move only slightly awkward as a result of his bulky boot. He lifted Truffles from Baz's lap. 'Ladies. Thank you for bringing this to my attention. I can assure you I will investigate these disturbing allegations. If I find out that what you're saying has any basis in reality, I'll be in touch.'

in which someone is in over their head

THINGS CARRIED on as normal for the next two days. Baz couldn't help but feel they were close to figuring things out – but the answers remained frustratingly out of reach.

On Monday evening, Peggy played a recording Baz had made of Mitch's voice. Tina was confident it wasn't him. The voice and accent were wrong, she said. Steve was American and his voice was smooth, whereas Mitch was very British and sounded like the ex-smoker he probably was.

Big Joe had said similar when Madge and Baz stopped by his to play the same recording for him on Tuesday afternoon.

On Wednesday, their tea and crafting session had been quiet thus far. Baz was working on a beautiful Northern Lights embroidery pattern.

They hadn't heard anything back from Mitch yet and they were at a dead end with all their other lines of enquiry.

Madge had finished the various pieces of the jumper she'd been working on. She had a very large yarn needle out and was stitching one of the sleeves to the bodice. Peggy was studying her screen. She'd received feedback on her next book from her beta readers. Now she needed to review the various points and decide on a strategy for the next draft. Carole was back to crochet – working on a severed human foot.

They normally worked until about half eleven, but at a few minutes past eleven, Baz was wondering whether it might be time to cut today's session short.

Suddenly, the room was filled with the tinny sounds of 'Ain't No Mountain High Enough'. It played for a few seconds and then stopped. 'Excuse me.' Madge reached into her bag and pulled out her ancient mobile phone. She tapped in her passcode and squinted at the screen.

'Well?' Peggy glared at her friend. 'I know you normally put that thing on silent – so I assume that's something to do with the case. Don't keep us in suspense.'

Baz decided it was a good time to start packing up her embroidery. Carole tapped on the window and whispered at a pigeon pecking for crumbs.

'Very interesting.' Madge looked up from her phone. 'That was a text from Mitch. He said he still doesn't know much about the business in question or who the seller is. But he was able to get us the address.'

'And?' Peggy slid her laptop into its sleeve. 'Where are we headed? Do I need to pop home first to grab my scooter?'

Madge chuckled. 'The address is on Deptford Broadway.'

Baz paused what she was doing. Her head was between her knees as she'd been putting her handiwork back into her bag. She looked up. 'But that's right there!'

Peggy was encouraging Carole to pack her crochet materials away. She looked back at Madge. 'Which number?'

'Thirty-two.' Madge's eyebrows were elevated as she looked at Peggy.

'But that's—' Peggy said at the same time as Baz said 'Isn't that—'

Neither woman finished her sentence.

'Exactly.' Madge stood up and waited while the others gathered their things.

Five minutes later, Baz parked her scooter on the wide pavement in front of the shop. Madge pushed open the door and the four women plus Cookie walked in.

Jimi's grin lit his whole face when he came towards them. 'Madge! Ladies, how lovely to see you. How can I help you this fine morning? Let me see if I can help you find your next favourite read. I told you I have a special skill for picking books people will enjoy. Let me see if—'

Madge put a hand on his arm. 'That's not why we're here, Jimi.'

His face fell before he tried a more tentative smile. 'Oh, is this a social call, then?'

Peggy was bent slightly forwards, studying the titles on a particular shelf. She stood back upright. 'We understand you're selling a business.' Cookie looked up at her, but remained sitting.

Jimi blinked. 'You mean I'm in the business of selling? That's not a secret.' He backed up to allow them all further into the shop, motioning at the shelves of books surrounding him.

In one corner stood a brown corduroy sofa and a striped velour wingback chair. Between the two there was a sturdy-looking coffee table with a few dings. The setup was mismatched and some of the pieces may have seen better days – but it looked warm, comfortable, and inviting.

'No,' Madge said. 'We have reason to believe that you are actively seeking a buyer for one of your businesses.'

'What?' Jimi walked back to his front counter and took his place behind it. 'I've only just opened my shop. It hasn't had a chance to prove itself yet.'

Baz stepped into the space he'd vacated. 'Not this business. You have another business – don't you, Jimi? One you didn't declare on your application for the lease of this place.'

Carole dropped herself into the armchair. She opened her bag and removed her crochet materials. Peggy released Cookie's lead and he walked over to Carole and lay down by her feet.

Jimi picked up a stack of papers and jogged them to tidy the edges. 'I'm sorry – I don't know what you're talking about.'

Madge walked to the counter and placed her hands on the worktop. 'Someone is selling an existing business that operates from this shop. A business that is engaged in very bad activities. *Illegal* activities.'

Jimi looked from Madge to Baz and back again. 'I wouldn't. It's not me.'

Madge pulled her phone from her handbag and clicked a few buttons. She turned the screen to face him. 'This is your address – is it not?'

'This is 32 Deptford Broadway,' he said as he squinted at the screen. 'Is that what it says?'

Baz felt her face scrunch up as she peered at Madge's phone. 'Unit 1a? This is unit 1. What's 1a?'

Jimi's face blanched. 'Oh.' He put a hand to his mouth. 'Oh.'

Peggy, who'd been studying the books on a shelf near the back wall, stepped into the conversation. 'What do you know?'

'Please, Jimi,' said Baz. 'This is important. People are being hurt.'

'Hurt?' Jimi looked like he was going to faint. 'No, no, no. They said there was nothing like that. Only storage. It's only storage.'

'Is there a kettle?' Baz looked around the room. She'd visited it before letting it out – but it looked quite different now. 'You look like you could do with a cup of tea.'

Jimi waved at a doorway behind the counter. 'Through

there.' He walked to the front door and flipped the lock. Then he grabbed a paper sign and affixed it to the door.

Baz followed Peggy through the doorway to the cupboard-sized office. This had been open to the main room when Baz had visited previously. There was a small fridge and a kettle near one wall. There was only one mug but Baz managed to find a sleeve of paper cups. The two of them made tea for four and a cup of instant coffee for Peggy.

When they carried the cups through to the main room, Cookie looked up at them, a big, silly grin on his face. Madge was squatting on the floor in front of Jimi, who was sitting on the sofa, trying not to weep. No, Baz realised. Madge wasn't squatting – she was sitting on a small stool. Baz had no idea where she'd found it. But she seemed to be comforting Jimi.

Baz handed Jimi the mug of tea she was carrying. He accepted it with thanks. He didn't drink it, though – just held it in trembling hands. He stared into the liquid.

Baz and Peggy distributed the other drinks. Peggy pointed to an assortment of folding chairs. They each took one and sat facing Jimi.

Madge moved from the little stool to the armchair. 'Now, Jimi. While my friends were making tea, you started to tell me something. Can you please tell us the whole story? Start at the beginning.'

Jimi inhaled slowly, then took a sip of the tea. 'This shop – it's always been this dream in the back of my head – I wasn't lying about that. But I never thought it would be reality. I've worked for forty years. I was a bus driver for TfL.'

Transport for London was responsible for all the city's trains, trams, and buses. They even managed many of the bicycles available for hire.

Jimi paused while he drank some more of his tea. When

Peggy looked at Baz, she responded with a small shrug. They needed to give him time to tell his story in his way.

After a few minutes, he continued. 'About eighteen months ago, I had a heart attack while driving the bus. No, I mean, it wasn't a heart attack – but I thought it was. I pulled the bus over safely. No one was injured. Some of the passengers were pretty annoyed at first but everyone was very kind once they realised what was going on.'

Baz had no idea where this story was heading. Peggy was making – thankfully subtle – rolling motions with her hands, silently urging Jimi to get to the point.

'As I say, I thought it was a heart attack – but the paramedics were able to confirm it wasn't that. But they still insisted on taking me to hospital. The doctors poked me, prodded me, and scanned me all day.'

Madge inhaled sharply. 'Angina.'

Baz was pretty sure that was a heart condition of some sort, though she didn't know why Madge reacted as though that explained anything.

'Yes.' Jimi looked at Madge. 'How did you guess?'

'Nurse practitioner,' Madge said.

'Ah, I see.' Jimi set the empty mug down on the low table. 'So you understand the implication?'

Madge looked at her friends. 'He lost his driving licence.' Turning back to face Jimi, she added, 'That's right – isn't it?'

He nodded.

Well, that explained part of the story at least.

'I got an insurance payout on top of my pension.' In his lap, Jimi's hands folded and unfolded – he was flexing and bending his fingers like he needed something to occupy them. 'But I didn't feel ready to retire. I really wasn't lying when I said this shop had been my dream.'

Baz uncrossed her legs and recrossed them the other way.

She was still missing something. Jimi seemed to be circling in on the matter, though.

'I always wanted to go into business for myself.' Jimi shrugged and looked at his shoes. They were alligator print with pointy toes. 'But I didn't know how hard it would be. I don't think I understood what I was getting myself into. So much time and effort – with not much to show for it.'

Peggy's eyebrows lifted. There was no doubt in Baz's mind now: they were getting closer.

'The money I got from the insurance paid for the deposit on this place. I was able to cover my first order of books – but the bills from the renovation work were starting to come due. And I had to pay rent on this place, plus my home. And all the bills.'

Cookie looked up at him but didn't move from Carole's side.

He looked away. When he spoke, there was a hitch in his voice. 'I was in over my head. Too many bills, not enough money coming in. I don't know – I guess I thought I'd start earning money right away.'

Peggy frowned. 'What did you do, Jimi?'

He shifted in his chair and chewed on his lip. 'I received a message from someone – oh Lord forgive me! I'm going to lose everything.' At this, Cookie stood up and walked over to the man and settled himself at Jimi's feet.

Madge placed a hand on his knee. 'Jimi, we need to know what happened.'

Jimi sniffed, then nodded. He wasn't looking away anymore – but he also wouldn't look the women in the eye. 'The cellar. Someone wanted to rent the cellar room. They didn't... I should've... They came at night. And now they've stopped paying. They disappeared – no response to my messages. You say there's something illegal happening. They're probably storing drugs in my cellar. That's what it is – isn't it? The cops are going to come in here and find them and I'll be the one left holding the bag. Oh Lord! I can't go to prison.' His breathing was increasing in pace.

Peggy rolled her eyes. 'Who was it?'

'I don't know,' Jimi said. 'They contacted me by text and paid by PayPal. I never met them – I've no idea who it is. They said they only needed to rent the space.'

'We should find out what's down there.' It finally dawned on Baz that she owned the building. 'Do you have the keys, Jimi? Because if not, I'm sure I do.'

'I do.' Jimi waved a hand at her. 'But they've added a padlock on the outside of the door. I don't have keys for that.'

Peggy pulled herself to her feet. 'Looks like we're going to need a pair of bolt cutters.'

Jimi looked up at Peggy. 'What are you going to do?'

She chuckled. 'What do you think we're going to do? We're cutting open that lock.'

Jimi tensed. 'And if it's drugs?'

Peggy shook her head. 'It's not going to be drugs.'

'No?' Jimi blinked. 'What is it then?'

'We don't know,' Madge said.

Jimi scratched his head. 'What?'

Baz stood up too. 'Someone's trying to frame us for— We're being set up.'

Jimi looked up at her. 'I don't understand.'

Madge, her hand still on his knee, added, 'Neither do we.'

'I think that's why we all need to know what's going on,' said Peggy.

Baz ran her hands down the soft chiffon fabric of her skirt. 'Someone's targeting us. Setting us up to make it look as though we're committing crimes. I think you're just, shall we say, collateral damage. But we really do need to get to the bottom of this. Please, Jimi.'

He sat for a moment, staring at the floor. 'All right. I've got my toolbox here somewhere. I hired a joiner to do the carpentry – but I did the plumbing and electrics myself.' He pulled himself to his feet and walked over to the counter. He disappeared through the door to the back room.

The sound of a door opening and closing was followed by the thud of something heavy being set down. The women looked at one another as they waited for Jimi to return.

After a few minutes, he reappeared, holding a large pair of bolt cutters in one hand. 'All right. Let's find out what's down there.'

There were three units in the building and each one came with a storeroom in the cellar. Jimi and Madge descended the steep staircase with ease. With their respective mobility issues, Baz and Peggy took their time. When they got to the bottom, Jimi had cut the bolt from the door.

As Jimi removed the broken lock from the door, Madge pushed it open. Baz thought she caught a muffled noise. 'Wait!'

But Jimi and Madge had already disappeared into the room. Baz couldn't see what they could, but she could've sworn she heard voices that didn't belong to any of the people with them. She and Peggy exchanged a glance – just as Madge called out, 'I need some help in here.'

in which a shocking discovery is made

PEGGY HAD NEVER BEEN A RUNNER – and especially not now with the state of her hips. But she knew Madge wouldn't call for help without good reason. So Peggy ran. She was pleased to note that Baz kept up with her. The pair pushed past Jimi, who was spraying something from a small bottle into his mouth. His heart meds, she assumed.

Peggy wasn't sure what she expected to find in this small room – but she wasn't prepared for what she actually encountered.

The smell alone almost knocked Peggy on her arse. She lifted a hand to her face as she fought to keep from gagging. The stench was overwhelming.

The room was lit by a single overhead fluorescent fixture. Along one wall, there stood an industrial-looking bunk bed. On the bottom bunk, a person sat cross-legged cradling the head of another person. 'Please,' he said. 'She needs help.' His accent was American – like someone who'd learnt English from TV and films.

The opposite wall had a long table – one of the cheap

folding ones you got for temporary meeting spaces. There were two mismatched bedraggled office chairs in front of it. In the far corner, there was a janitor's sink. On one wall hung a partially finished drawing of a German shepherd dog who looked strangely like Cookie. As she stepped closer, she realised it wasn't a drawing – it was needlework.

Peggy wasn't sure how long the pair had been trapped down here, but she guessed this was all they'd had access to for all their needs. That single sink was serving as kitchen, shower, and toilet.

With one hand, Madge grabbed one of the well-used wheelie chairs and rolled it over to the bed, dropping herself into it. She began examining the woman. With a nod, she flung her hand out behind herself. 'Get me my kit – I'll take the stethoscope first, please.'

Even Peggy could see the girl wasn't in a good way. She could hear her wheezing from where she stood. Peggy couldn't make out what she was whispering – couldn't even hear enough to tell what language it was.

Madge turned back to the girl and spoke: 'Soy enfermera. Mi amiga me traerá mi ... er, she'll hand me my ... er ... supplies.'

Still wheezing, the girl nodded.

Peggy snatched the bag from the doorway, where Madge had dropped it. She hauled it over to the desk next to... Wait. Was that her old laptop? The top was emblazoned with a host of music and political stickers – including a pink one featuring a clown on a unicycle and the words 'mock the patriarchy'.

What on earth was it doing here? Well, that was certainly something she'd need to think about – just not right now.

Jimi had his phone in his hands. 'I'll just—'

'No!' Multiple people shouted the word at once, but the most fervent was the young man. His voice was rasping and scratchy. 'Please, no! No police.' He lapsed into a language Peggy wasn't familiar with and repeatedly genuflected. Something Asian, she suspected. Whatever the language, it was obvious he was praying.

Peggy handed Madge the stethoscope. Madge accepted it without a word and continued her exam.

Baz took the young man by the hand and guided him to the other office chair. He struggled to walk. 'It's okay. My friend is a nurse. No one will call the police if you don't want us to. We only want to make sure you're all right. My name's Baz. Can I ask what your name is?'

He was young – probably only in his early twenties. He was roughly the same height as Peggy and Baz – average height or maybe a bit on the short side for a man. And so thin. He had dull, sunken eyes. 'Reyn.'

'Sorry?' Baz clearly found that as confusing as Peggy did. Was he asking about the weather?

'My name,' he said. 'It's Reynaldo. But I like Reyn.' He sounded like he'd smoked several packs of cigarettes just this morning. 'Marta's inhaler ran out a few days ago.'

'Are you okay, Reyn?' Baz studied the boy. 'Sorry, you're clearly not okay. I mean ... sorry. I only want to help. We didn't know...'

'There should be an asthma inhaler in my kit.' Madge held her hand out. Peggy fumbled in the bag until she found it.

She turned her attention back to Reyn as soon as she'd handed over the inhaler. 'What my friend means is that we didn't know there was anyone down here.'

'How long...' Baz's words trailed off as she looked around the room.

The boy looked like he was going to faint. 'We've been here for about three months. But they stopped bringing food a few days ago.'

Peggy's eyes widened. 'You haven't eaten?'

Reyn shook his head. 'It used to come through there.' He waved a hand at the door. His hands were swollen and bloody and his movements were slow, languid. 'There's a little ... thingy.' He reverted to his first language. Maybe it was Tagalog? 'A little door. They put food and supplies there.'

While Reyn was talking, Baz had whispered something to Jimi, who turned and left the room.

In a weak voice, the girl Madge was still helping shouted, 'No a la policía!'

Jimi paused with his hand on the door frame. 'No police. You have my word. I'll only be a minute.'

As Jimi left the room, Reyn hobbled back to the bunk bed where Madge was still with his friend. 'How are you feeling, Marta?' He turned to the women. 'She understands English – but she's not confident in speaking it.'

The girl – Marta – seemed weak but she smiled when she looked up. She was sitting with her back to the wall. 'Mejor. Better. Seniora Dixon ... give me ... medicamento.'

'Thank you.' He lowered himself to the bed and leant against his friend.

Madge pushed her glasses up and gestured towards his hands. 'May I?' He nodded, so she took his hands in hers and examined them. 'I'm going to need—'

'No hospital! No police!' He pulled his hands away from her.

Madge raised her own hand in a placating gesture. 'No hospitals, I promise. But I need more supplies. Medicine. Better lighting. You've got deep abrasions. And your left hand is showing signs of infection.'

Baz walked up behind Madge and put a hand on her friend's shoulder. 'Something's happened to his right foot too,' she whispered. 'I think he might've been kicking the door.'

Madge nodded. 'Marta, I'd like to take you and your friend

here to my home. A mi casa. Will you let me? I have food there. And medicine.'

Before the girl could answer, Jimi returned. He held two cups of tea and a sleeve of biscuits. 'It was all I had. Sorry. I figured it was better than nothing.' How very British. Peggy wasn't entirely sure what was happening but she knew it was going to take more than tea to fix this.

The two kids almost pounced on Jimi. Reyn grimaced when he touched the hot paper cup. Jimi stepped forwards and held it for him, allowing Reyn to drink without doing further injury to his wounded hands.

Marta tore open the packet of biscuits and ate slowly and carefully. 'Gracias. Thank you.' She handed a stack to Reyn, who wolfed them down.

When they had devoured all the biscuits, Marta looked at Reyn. 'We go with her.' Her voice was soft and laboured, like every word took effort.

They looked at each other for several heartbeats before Reyn answered. 'Okay. It can't be any worse than here.'

'You're going to need help getting them upstairs.' Peggy turned to Baz. 'We'd only get in the way. I'll send Carole down to assist.'

Madge nodded.

As the two women made their way carefully up the stairs, Peggy said, 'Will you be all right to walk if you let the kids ride your scooter? The alternative is I go home and fetch mine. Neither one of them is in any kind of state to walk to Madge's.'

Baz paused on the step above Peggy. 'I'm not sure they're up to driving either.' She started moving again.

'Fair point.' Peggy grimaced as her hip joint ground itself painfully.

Baz made it to the top of the stairs and paused for another quick breather. 'I'll ring for a cab.'

They waited twenty minutes for the taxi. The driver hadn't been keen on taking them once he got a whiff of the two kids – but Madge told him in no uncertain terms that she didn't think that was very charitable. And Baz assured him there would be a hefty tip in it for him. Madge, Jimi, and the two young people got in the taxi and departed.

Peggy joined Carole and Cookie on foot, with Baz accompanying them on the scooter. Their pace was infuriatingly slow. Peggy cursed her ancient hips. But – thanks to the one-way streets and the turning restrictions – they managed to get to Madge's a full minute before the cab did.

Madge helped Marta up the stairs to Madge's front door while Carole and Jimi supported Reyn so he could hop without putting too much weight on his injured foot.

'One thing I don't understand,' Peggy said as she and Baz made their way slowly up the stairs. She fought the instinct to curl up in the stairwell for a nap. 'How did no one in that building hear what was happening? I suspect that's how Reyn ended up so injured – kicking and clawing at the door. It's what I would have done.'

'The little door for the food wasn't the only thing added to that room.' Baz's words had a staccato quality as she focused on getting up the stairs. 'They could have had a heavy metal concert down there – no one would have noticed with all the soundproofing that was in there.'

'Ah, I hadn't spotted that,' Peggy said as they paused on the landing that marked the halfway point.

Baz put her hand on the handrail to begin the next set of stairs. 'You know what else I noticed in that room?'

'My missing laptop?' Peggy put her foot on the first step.

Baz cocked her head in acknowledgement. 'And my stolen phone.' She lifted her hand from her pocket and waved the device in question. 'Oh, plus my embroidery.'

That explained the picture of Cookie Peggy had seen. 'Oh! I didn't spot your phone. I did ask Carole to grab my laptop, though.'

Just then Carole appeared at the top of the stairs. 'Oh, there you are, love. I've been meaning to talk to you about the internet. It's been very noisy lately – don't you find?'

Peggy reached the top of the stairs and took her lover's offered arm. After a moment, Baz joined them and they made their way along the walkway to Madge's front door.

They found everyone in Madge's cluttered guest room. The two young people were lying on the room's double bed. Marta had one of those oxygen-measurement devices clamped onto her right index finger. Madge had Reyn's sock off and was inspecting his swollen foot. It was so filthy that Peggy struggled to tell whether there was any discolouration.

Madge flexed the ankle while Reyn flinched and yelped. Madge grimaced as she turned to Baz. 'Call Cheryl. If she's not available, try Moses. He's a pharmacist.' She raised a hand as she looked back at the patients on the bed. 'I promise – no police or hospitals. I'm calling my daughter. She's a nurse too.' Looking back at Baz, she added, 'Tell her to send salbutamol, prednisolone, amoxycillin, oxycontin. I've got some here, but we're going to need more today.'

Reyn and Marta both visibly relaxed.

Madge touched Reyn on the shoulder. 'You're safe now. I promise. My friends and I will get you some food. If you'd like to get cleaned up in the meantime, I'll show you where the bathroom is. I'm sure I can find you some clean clothes to put on.'

Both kids sat up. 'Thank you.' They looked at each other.

'I think I'd like to have a bath, if I could,' Reyn said.

Marta nodded.

Peggy assumed they'd want to use the facilities separately. But both young people hauled themselves up at the same time.

Madge pulled a cane from heaven only knew where and handed it to Reyn. 'Baz, fetch them some towels from that chest of drawers, would you, dear?' She ushered the kids to the bathroom. 'When you're done, just leave your dirty clothes on the floor. We'll put them in the wash. You should find something to wear in the same drawers Baz got the towels from. Help yourself to whatever suits.'

Once the kids were ensconced in the bathroom, Madge took Jimi's hands in her own. 'Thank you, Olujimi. We are grateful for your help today.'

'Of course. It would be inhumane to do anything else. And I feel awful for my role in ... in...' He swallowed. 'I would never knowingly...'

Madge squeezed his hands. 'I know that, Jimi. You're a good man.'

'I'm so sorry. If there's anything I can do, please – you only have to call me.'

'Thank you.' Madge smiled at him. 'Now you'd best get back to your shop. I'll ring you later – I promise.'

Jimi nodded, waved farewell to the other women, and left.

Peggy followed Madge to the flat's tiny kitchen. They sent Baz, Carole, and Cookie through to the lounge to keep them from getting under foot.

Madge scooped leftover plantain curry and rice onto two plates. She handed the first one to Peggy. 'Put that in the microwave, would you? About three minutes each.'

Peggy did so. 'Well. What's your diagnosis, nurse?'

Madge reached into the cupboard and pulled out two tall glasses. 'Reyn has a badly bruised foot and an infected laceration on his hand. I don't think anything's broken, though – praise the Lord. Marta has chronic asthma. Her inhaler ran out a few days ago. Both should recover in a matter of weeks at most.' She removed a jug of cloudy liquid from the fridge and filled both glasses. 'Well, at least physically.'

When the bell sounded, Peggy took the first plate from the microwave and swapped it for the second. 'I can't imagine the psychological effects of being held captive for so long.'

'Mmm.' Madge nodded as she picked out cutlery from the drawer. 'Indeed. Marta told me they'd both been removed from the immigration detention centres. They thought they were being deported. But then there was a dodgy handover to someone in a van with blacked out windows. She thinks they were both singled out because of their skills. Reyn for his English and her for her tech skills.'

When the microwave pinged a second time, Peggy took the plate out. They gathered everything up and brought it to the spare room, ready for when the kids returned from getting cleaned up.

wherein baz has a realisation

THE REST of the week passed in relative calmness. Baz knew it was the calm before the storm – but there wasn't anything they could do just yet. The two kids were doing as well as could be expected, so that was positive. Marta had been the one handling the tech side of things. Reyn had been posing as the elusive Steve on the long phone calls with his victims.

Well, not *his* victims, as such. Those two kids were suffering every bit as much as Tina and Big Joe and the rest.

But the women were still missing that final clue that would crack the case wide open. Who was behind this scheme? Why were she and Peggy being framed?

Outside of morning coffee meetings with the girls, Baz devoted most of her time to research. Or rather, to be more accurate, she spent her time performing the same searches over and over again in the hopes that this time, she might uncover something. But of course she never did. She'd passed some details over to a friend in the RCMP. They had access to resources that Baz no longer did. But she hadn't heard back yet.

'What's wrong, sweet pea?'

Startled out of her reverie, Baz looked up into Paul's warm amber eyes. 'I'm sorry, mister. I've been a million miles away. What were you saying?' The balcony door was open behind him, allowing a warm summer breeze to waft through the flat.

Paul turned the linguini on his plate around his fork, using his spoon for support in the classic Italian way. 'I was telling you about a library customer this morning who— You know what? It doesn't matter. It was only a throwaway story. It feels like there's something weighing on your mind. You can talk to me, you know.'

Paul had finally come over for dinner. He'd done the cooking, with Baz playing sous chef – just like she used to do for Hari. Oh, Hari! Why did she have to start thinking about him again? Now of all times!

'I...' She started, then stumbled over her words. 'I'm so sorry, Paul. I know I can. You're such a good man and I—'

Paul lifted his napkin from his lap and dabbed his lips. 'That sounds like there's a *but* coming.'

'No, I...' Baz pressed her fist to her lips. 'I'm sorry. There's a lot going on right now and I—'

He reached across the table and placed his hand gently atop hers – well, atop the one that wasn't still pressed to her face. 'So talk to me. It's what I'm here for, sweet pea. Whatever it is, you know I'll understand.'

Baz lowered her left hand and placed it atop Paul's. 'I don't deserve you, mister.'

Paul frowned. 'Oh, sweet pea. Everyone deserves a second chance at happiness. What's brought this on?'

She knew she couldn't tell him about everything. Could she trust him enough to tell him about Reyn and Marta or would that lead to questions about what she and her friends were going to do about the culprit when they found him? As she focused on what bits she could and couldn't tell him, her mouth seemed to make a decision of its own accord. 'It's Hari.'

Oh dear. She hadn't meant to say that. Where had it come from?

Paul's brow furrowed. 'Hari, your ex-husband Hari? What's he done?'

Before she could stop herself, it all came tumbling out. 'He called me last week. Just out of the blue. Told me he missed me. We ended up talking all night. It felt so good to talk to him again, *really* talk, and I—'

Paul withdrew his hand from hers. 'I see.' The hurt in his eyes stabbed her in the guts. He pushed his chair away from the table. He smiled, but there was so much sadness in the look that it broke Baz. 'I should get going.'

She reached out and took his hand in hers. The questions that had been plaguing her for a week fell away. 'No, Paul. Please stay. Hear me out.'

With a crisp nod, he resumed his seat. 'I'm listening.' He didn't take her hand but his eyes were filled with sympathy.

'Hari and I have been talking lately. It's … nice.' Up until this very minute, she hadn't been sure where her heart lay. But the moment she'd mentioned Hari's name, it had all become crystal clear in her mind and now she needed to get it all out before she ruined everything. 'Hari and I were married for twenty years and together for a decade before that.'

Paul's lips tightened and his eyes narrowed.

'But before that, we were friends for a decade. He wasn't just my husband – my partner. He was also my best friend. Not having him in my life for this past year has been … difficult. And from our conversations this week, I know he feels the same.'

When Paul swallowed, Baz could tell she was losing him. She reached across the table and took his hand. 'I've missed his friendship. And I hope that he and I have made some progress towards rebuilding it out of the ashes of our marriage. But my future isn't with him – it's with you. If you'll still have me.'

A tear dropped from Paul's eye as a grin spread across his face. 'Really?'

'Oh, don't you start – you'll get me going.' Baz brushed a tear from her own eye. 'But yes, really.'

As they resumed their dinner, the truth came pouring out of her. 'I've been fretting so much lately, thinking I'm a fool for assuming I could have something new at my age.'

Paul paused with his fork raised halfway to his mouth. 'At our age, you mean.'

'Touché.' Baz smiled softly.

'Because I *do* think you can have something new.' He set the fork down and touched her hand briefly. 'I believe you deserve to have something new, Barbara Lorraine Spencer. It would be awfully unfair of me to think otherwise – given that I also happen to think *I* deserve to have something new.'

'We may not have our whole lives in front of ourselves anymore—'

Paul raised a hand to stop her. 'Hey, now. Excuse me. I've got a good few decades left in me.'

Baz grinned. 'Naturally. As do I. What I meant is that we're not twenty years old anymore. We don't have forever—'

'No one does!' He shook his head. '*No one* is promised a long life.'

'That's true enough.' Baz released a sigh. She felt more at ease than she had in months.

The candle on the table was reflected in Paul's glasses and in his eyes. There was silence as they both ate a bit more of the delicious meal he'd prepared. 'I don't know where our relationship is going to go in the long term. But after four months, I can promise you this, sweet pea. I'm not going anywhere any time soon. Unless you want me to, of course. It would break my heart but I'd respect your decision.'

Warmth flooded Baz's insides. A rush of happiness flowed through her body, touching all her extremities. 'Nothing would make me happier than continuing to explore life with you, Hilary Paul Brown. I've been second-guessing myself for the last week. And triple-guessing and whatever comes after that. It's made me absolutely miserable.'

She picked up her napkin and folded it before setting it on the table, next to her plate. 'For the longest time – before I met you, I mean – I thought I wanted Hari to admit he was wrong to let me go. It's funny because I didn't want to leave my new life in London. But at the same time, I also wanted to slot back into my old life in Edmonton.'

Paul picked up the bottle of merlot in the middle of the table and topped up both their glasses. She thought he might say something, but when he didn't, she continued.

'And then I met you and there was this instant spark – a connection I never thought I'd have again. You make me so happy, Paul. And I think it made me feel a funny sort of guilt. It was like I was cheating on Hari. Not the *real* Hari. It was more like I was cheating on the version of him that only existed in my mind after we split up. I had this fantasy of him where—'

She cut herself off and took a sip of her wine. 'I told you why we divorced, didn't I?'

Paul nodded. 'When you told him you wanted to live as the woman you are, he couldn't cope.'

Baz nodded. 'He was very good about it. Supportive. Lovely. But at the same time, he said he was a gay man and that he couldn't ever envision a point in his life where he'd want to be with a woman. It hurt – it tore me apart. At one point – okay, probably at many points – I said to him, "It's still me. I'm a woman and I always have been. So when you say you can't be with a woman, I have news for you."'

She laughed despite the ache in her chest. 'Once, he replied by saying, "Yeah, but you know what I mean." That was the point where I packed my bag and left. Even still, the divorce was never bitter. Always amicable. It stung. But I understood – or at least I tried to.'

She stood up and cleared away the dinner plates. 'But in my head, the relationship continued. Or it picked up where it left off. Only in my mind, of course.'

Paul followed her through to the kitchen side of the room. They stacked the dishes next to the sink.

Baz removed the little mousse pots from the fridge and carried them through to the table. 'I allowed myself the fantasy version where he confessed he was wrong and begged me to come back. And so, in my head, there was always this little voice telling me that being with you was cheating on him. It's stupid and childish and—'

Paul gave her a warm and loving smile as he placed his hand in hers under the table. 'And completely normal. But I think we should eat this delicious mousse before it softens and melts.'

For the next few minutes, they ate in silence. When they had dinner together, Baz normally prepared a baked dessert, since she could bake but not cook. But Paul had wanted to make all the food for tonight's meal. The mousse was incredible – light and creamy but with a rich chocolatey flavour.

'And then he called me and we ended up talking all night. It felt so easy, so natural to slip back into his life. To be honest, I really hope it continues. He's a lovely man and I want the absolute best for him. But what I've realised tonight is that the relationship I have with Hari now is friendship. We're family. I have two beautiful stepdaughters because of him. We have four lovely grandkids – two on his side and two on mine – and a host of extended family.'

She set the empty mousse cup down and took a sip of the wine. Baz was far from a wine expert but she thought the merlot worked just as well with it as it had with the pasta. 'I've really enjoyed the conversations I've had with Hari this past week. And I've felt so conflicted over them. But it wasn't until tonight that I've realised – I don't need to be conflicted.'

Baz stretched her arm across the small table and took Paul's hand. 'The Hari that existed in my head for the past two years isn't the one I've been talking to for the last few days. Because that Hari never existed. He wasn't real. I'm always going to love the real Harendra Sharma but I'm not *in love* with him. Not anymore.'

She took a breath before continuing. 'I love *you*, mister.'

Paul fanned his face with his hands. 'And I love you, sweet pea. You don't know how long I've been waiting to say that. I didn't want to be the first to say it. I didn't want to let myself get hurt. Not again.'

Just then, Baz's phone let out a sharp trill. 'Oh, I'm sorry, Paul. I was sure I'd turned that off.' She stood up to look for it to shut it off. And that's when she caught sight of the screen. 'No, sorry. I need to take this one. I'm so sorry, love. Please, I'll be as quick as I can.'

She did put it on silent. But she'd set it to make an exception for Shirley, her friend in the RCMP. She got to it just in time. 'Shirley?'

'Hiya, Baz. Have I caught you at a good time?' The person who appeared on-screen was a round-faced woman with long black hair. She had a Newfie accent. Shirley had moved from Gander to Edmonton several decades back but never lost the distinctive Irish-sounding brogue.

'I, er... It's fine, Shirley. How are you?' Baz ducked into the bedroom to take the call.

'Oh, you know. Same old, same old. The kids have the flu and the dog's been asked not to come back to the daycare. Kelly's had a promotion at his job, though, so we've got a little bit more money to play with these days. What about you, Baz? You're all dolled up – have I interrupted something important? How's life in jolly old London?'

Baz couldn't help the smile that spread across her face and warmed her insides. 'You know what, Shirl? I'm very well, thanks. Now... What have you got for me?'

'Right to business, then? All right. I can do that – but you owe me some good gossip later, girl.'

'Fair enough,' Baz replied.

'Okay, I dug into the details of those company names and accounts you sent me earlier. Now, I have to ask – are you testing me, girl? Just trying to check I've still got it?' The background moved as Shirley spun around in her chair – Baz could hear it squeaking as she did so. It was a habit the younger woman had had for as long as they'd known one another.

'I don't understand.' Baz shook her head.

'Well, a couple of the accounts belonging to this company are in your name.' Shirley grimaced. 'Um, I mean your dead-name. A joint account with—' Shirley stopped spinning and squinted at something. 'Do you know anyone by the name of Margaret Persephone Trent? Ooh, are you on a date with her right now?'

Baz chuckled. 'Her partner would murder me if I were.' She made it sound like a joke, though Baz suspected her words were *literally* true.

'Ah, okay.' Shirley resumed spinning.

'So it was a dead end, then?' Baz frowned. She'd really thought Shirley would crack the case wide open for them.

Shirley wagged a finger. 'Ah, not so fast, my friend. The bank accounts are in your names. But I was able to get some details on the company names. And here's where it gets interesting.' She bobbled her head. 'More interesting, I mean.'

'How so?'

'Well...' Shirley dragged the word out. 'Remember those companies you had me look into for you a few months ago, yeah?'

'I know, I know,' Baz said. 'I still owe you dinner. I'm planning to come out for a week or so in September. I promise—'

Baz had no idea how Shirley didn't fall off the spinning chair when she waved a hand. 'No, no. That's not what I mean. It would be great to see you, though. And there's a new Ethiopian place I've been dying to try. You know how Kelly feels about spicy food, so I need someone to go with. No, what I mean is – it's the same owner. What was it? You Brits have the funniest names. Casper something.'

A chill ran down Baz's spine. 'Crispin Caspian Todd-Mitchell?'

'Aye, that's the one.'

in which the weather turns

BAZ SPENT most of the weekend with Paul – when she and her friends weren't trying to come up with a plan, that is. The texts flew back and forth.

One, in particular, stood out in Baz's mind.

MADGE

You ladies are not going to believe what the kids just told me.

Several minutes passed before there was another message. Baz looked eagerly at her screen.

PEGGY

We certainly won't if you don't tell us.

MADGE

I don't type as quickly as you. This infernal device is too fiddly. Be patient!

BAZ

It's fine, Madge. We'll wait.

In truth, she wasn't feeling especially patient. But arguing with Madge wouldn't make her type any faster. Eventually, the response came.

Instead of a text, the video message icon popped up. Baz clicked to play.

Madge's face appeared. She wore a purple satin sleep bonnet. 'Early on in their confinement, their captor brought food and supplies himself. He always wore a balaclava so they couldn't see his face, though. But one day when he came to make a drop-off, Marta charged at him with one of the chairs. Broke his foot. After that, food was only ever pushed through the little slot.'

Before Baz had even finished playing the video, the phone buzzed again.

PEGGY

Gee, if only we knew someone with a broken foot.

The women had their final planning session on Sunday night at Peggy and Carole's. On Monday, they met as usual for their morning tea session. For the most part, they sat quietly and worked on their crafts. Though, internally, Baz's mind was awhirl with what would come next.

When it was time to head out, the women packed up their belongings. Marta and Reyn walked into the café's second room. She held their coffees. He still walked on crutches – somehow, he also managed to carry a couple of shopping bags.

'Good morning, aunties.' Now that her asthma was under control, Marta seemed to be doing much better. Her English was improving by the day. Given how well she understood anything that was said to her, Baz suspected the issue was a confidence one.

The six of them exchanged greetings.

Baz loaded the last of her belongings into her handbag. 'It's good to see you both out and about. How are you feeling?' She felt her skin warm as she spoke the words. 'Sorry. I meant physically, that is. I'm sure the psychological effects will linger for a long time to come.'

Marta smiled, though there was a hauntedness to it. 'Much better physically, yes.'

Reyn set his crutches aside and settled into a chair at a nearby table. 'I reckon it'll be a long time before either of us wants to sleep with the door closed, though.' Cookie made his way over to the lad and plunked himself down on his feet.

Carole stood and offered an arm to help Peggy up.

Madge loaded her new knitting project into her handbag and stood up. 'They've been making excellent progress. And Cheryl found a therapist who's agreed to help them work through things.'

'That's good.' Baz pulled herself to her feet. 'Counselling is so beneficial.'

Peggy picked up Cookie's lead. 'What are you two up to today? Been to the shops?'

Reyn nodded. 'We promised Mrs Dixon we'd make dinner for her this evening, so we wanted to pick up a few ingredients before our appointment with the immigration lawyer.'

Marta stirred a packet of sugar into her coffee. 'He comes to the flat this afternoon to talk to Reyn and me.'

Peggy turned to Madge. 'Chuk?'

Madge nodded. Her ex-husband was a lawyer specialising in human rights cases.

'You'll like him,' Baz said. 'He's a lovely man.'

They made their farewells and headed out.

When the door closed behind them, the women clustered together beside the café, near Baz's scooter. Madge said, 'Based on what I've told him, he says he believes both the kids will be granted asylum on appeal. It sounds like there were technical errors in their first applications that he can rectify – and when you add to that the fact that they were kidnapped out of a government facility...' She kissed her teeth.

Baz removed the scooter's cover. It hadn't rained while they'd been in the café but it was still threatening to. The air felt heavy with it. 'I still can't get my head round that. Someone working in the detention centre *must* have been in on it.' She set her handbag down in the scooter's basket.

Madge rubbed her thumb and first two fingers together. 'A little bribery goes a long way.'

'I'd imagine what happened to them should help support their case, no?' Peggy looked at Madge.

Madge shifted her handbag from one arm to the other. 'I hope so. Chukwuma should be able to help them navigate the process.'

'Could Sarah perhaps give Marta a job? That would boost her confidence in her English.' Baz mounted her scooter and slid the key into the ignition.

'Not possible.' Madge wagged a finger. 'Asylum seekers can't be employed in this country. Not until they're granted asylum.'

'Disgraceful.' Peggy motioned towards her block of flats. 'Shall we?'

Instead of heading their separate ways, the four women set out on the short walk to Peggy and Carole's. They needed more privacy than they could rely on at either Baz's or Madge's.

As soon as Carole opened the door, the scents of garlic and cumin and tomatoes made Baz's mouth water. She waved a plastic container she'd been carting around. 'I've got the bread. Baked it fresh this morning.'

Baz had always loved baking but had only recently started trying her hand at bread. The first few loaves were okay but not great; however, the overnight recipe she'd found a few weeks ago had changed everything.

Peggy accepted the loaf from her before Cookie could grab it from Baz's hands. 'Thank you, dear. That'll go beautifully with the lentil soup I made. I threw all the ingredients into the slow cooker, so it should be just about ready.' She motioned to the cupboard. 'Are you all right to set the table?'

Baz washed her hands in the kitchen sink quickly before doing just that. Within minutes, the four women were sitting down to a very nice lunch.

As they ate, they ran through the plan for the afternoon. They all had their own roles to play, and it was vital they each knew what to do and when.

Once they'd cleaned up the dishes and Carole had delivered Cookie to their upstairs neighbours for the afternoon, the four women set out. Baz and Peggy were on their respective scooters; Carole and Madge were on foot.

Fifteen minutes – and some nervous chatter – later, they turned onto Elverson Road. It was a grey and miserable day, still threatening to rain. Once the mobility scooters had been parked and covered, Baz and Peggy joined their friends at the front door. Madge pressed the bell.

Truffles started barking immediately but a few moments passed before they heard Mitch bellowing. 'Hold yer horses. I ain't moving too quick!' After a minute, the door swung inwards. 'Oh. Ladies.' He stood aside with a smile. 'Come on in.'

Madge stepped forwards. 'We brought cake.'

'I'm sure it will be delicious.' Something about Mitch's grin made Baz shiver. 'I was wondering when I should expect you to show up again.'

'We'll make us all some tea, shall we?' Baz asked.

Mitch made to head for the kitchen. 'Excellent plan.'

Madge lifted a hand to stop him. 'You should rest that foot of yours. We'll take care of everything and join you in a few moments.'

He nodded. 'That's very kind. If you're sure, well, I'm not going to say no to that. We'll talk in the lounge today, I think. The weather's too grim to enjoy the garden.' He made his way from the front door to the living room, where he sat down on one of the light-blue velvet armchairs. Once he was settled, he propped his boot-clad foot on a teal ottoman. Carole joined him and made herself at home on the sofa.

Baz followed Madge and the others. The staircase was solid wood, with a beautiful banister. She made her way into the kitchen, noticing a small downstairs loo she hadn't spotted before. Truffles, clearly excited at the prospect of food, stuck close to her. She bent to give him a quick bit of fuss.

Madge already had the kettle on to boil by the time Baz got to the counter. She gave her hands a quick wash before joining Madge. 'What do you need me to do?'

Madge handed Baz a very fashionable Le Creuset teapot. 'I'll let you two make the tea while I plate up this cake.' She pointed Peggy towards the mugs in the cupboard.

Baz took a couple of teabags from the box of Yorkshire Tea she found in the cupboard. Mitch had a high-end espresso machine – but no decaf. 'Peggy, would you settle for hot chocolate?'

Madge had unwrapped her homemade Jamaican rum cake and sliced into it. 'She'll be fine.'

Peggy shook her head. 'I don't need you to speak for me, Madge. I'm right here.'

Madge waved a hand.

Peggy turned to Baz. 'Hot chocolate will be fine. Thank you.'

They couldn't find a tray, so the three women carried as much of the goodies as they could manage.

When they returned to the lounge, Carole was regaling Mitch with what Baz was pretty sure was the plot of *Reservoir Dogs*. Mitch smiled as though he thought he knew something she didn't.

Peggy joined Carole on the sofa. Madge motioned for Baz to take the remaining armchair before squeezing herself into the end of the sofa, next to Carole.

Mitch balanced the cake plate on the knee of his good leg as he lifted the tea to his lips. 'So, ladies. To what do I owe the pleasure of your company? And for the second time in a week at that.'

The glint in his eyes put Baz in mind of a predator, whose prey had just stepped into sight. But, she admitted to herself, she could be reading too much into it.

It was obvious he was framing them – her and Peggy specifically – for the romance fraud. But several things remained unclear. For one thing, why?

Unless it's as simple as revenge?

Six months before, the women had blackmailed him. They had uncovered a complex web of shell companies designed to perpetrate tax fraud. They'd used this information to suggest he might like to sell Baz a few of his properties to them at bargain-basement prices – or else they'd send the evidence to HMRC.

But the bigger question was the one Baz couldn't get her head around: what was his end goal?

'Baz?'

At the sound of Madge's voice, Baz felt her cheeks grow warm. 'My apologies. Could I ask you to repeat that last bit, please, dear?'

Madge gave a small shake of her head – Baz could tell it was taking effort to refrain from kissing her teeth. 'Peggy asked you to tell Mitch what you uncovered.'

'Sorry, yes, of course.' Baz touched a finger to her lips. 'As you know, we've been investigating a series of romance frauds with common threads running through them.'

'Yes, I'm aware. You'll recall I was one of the victims, after all. If I get my hands on that Steve...' Mitch shook his head.

Madge frowned, silently expressing the same suspicion Baz felt.

'Were you, though?' Peggy, on the other hand, wasn't one to keep her thoughts inside.

'Yeah.' Mitch gave a very sincere look. Baz wondered whether he practised it. 'Course I was. That's why I went to that support thing. To talk about my relationship with Steve.' He shook his head. 'My so-called relationship. With someone who called himself Steve. It's how I ended up calling you lot. You know that.'

'Mmm hmm.' Madge fixed him with a penetrating gaze. Baz knew that look; when Madge turned it on you, it felt like she was peering straight into your soul.

Mitch shrugged. 'What? Are you implying I'm not a victim? Aren't you lot always the ones telling people to "believe victims"?'

Baz felt her eyebrows arch upwards. Truffles, seemingly unaware of the tension in the room, was roaming around, hoovering up cake crumbs. When she smiled at him, he hopped lightly up into her lap.

Peggy scoffed. 'You son of a—'

Madge raised a hand and Peggy bit back the rest of her sentence. 'What my friend means is that we *do* believe victims – but you are not the victim here.'

'It's time to cut the crap, Mitch. Spino. Whatever you're

calling yourself this week. We're onto you.' Peggy crossed her arms over her chest.

Mitch sat very still, breathing slowly for several heartbeats. 'What do you think you know?' His voice contained a note of ... was that glee?

'Oh, I know a great many things.' Carole paused her knitting and looked up at Mitch. 'Most people have no idea. Not a clue. But I've studied the sacred texts. It all comes down to Princess Anne. They think she's just a plant by the Pope. But let me tell you, she's nothing of the sort. She's the one who helped me uncover...'

Baz tuned Carole out as she leant over and set her teacup on the side table because Truffles wouldn't stop trying to stick his face into it.

'We know *everything*,' Peggy said with a cocky grin.

'Ladies.' Mitch chuckled. The sound was low and warm. 'I'm afraid you have no idea who you're dealing with.'

Baz had to bite down on her lip to keep from laughing out loud. They knew more about him than he would ever know about them.

Peggy raised an eyebrow and fixed him with a stare. 'Do we not?' She turned to Madge. 'What does he think we don't know?'

Mitch bent over and slid open a drawer in the small table next to his chair. He retrieved a stack of manila folders and placed them on his lap before looking at each woman in turn. The look on his face was so smug that Baz's blood ran cold.

in which peggy and baz hide in the kitchen

MITCH LEANT BACK in his chair. 'Once upon a time, you ladies came to my home—'

This man really is insufferable, Peggy thought. Most of the time, she felt a smidgen of remorse when they had to take a life in the name of protecting their community. But right now, she figured she might enjoy seeing the life fade from his eyes.

Peggy set her empty mug on the coffee table. 'It was six months ago. Our minds are not so far gone that we've already forgotten.'

No, she wouldn't *enjoy* it. She may be a killer, but she wasn't that kind of killer. She wouldn't lose any sleep over it, though.

'You came into *my home*...' The last two words were so low Peggy had to strain to hear them. 'You thought you could force me to do your bidding by—'

Peggy made a show of rolling her eyes. 'I think you'll find we *did* persuade you to do our bidding, actually. There wasn't any tr—' This whole thing was just an elaborate revenge ploy. How tedious.

'I'm talking now.' Mitch didn't shout – he even spoke the

words with a smile. But hatred oozed out of his smarmy pores. 'You thought you had bested me. You're nothing but a trio of harmless little old ladies and one—'

'Don't you dare,' said both Peggy and Madge simultaneously.

'Baz is—' Peggy wagged her finger at Mitch.

She never did get to find out how she was going to finish that sentence.

Mitch chuckled as he waved a hand – not in Baz's direction but in Carole's. 'Three old ladies and one mindless—'

Peggy wanted to throttle him with her bare hands. But she didn't get the chance.

'Oh, good heavens. I don't think you're going to want to finish that sentence, kitten,' Carole said, without looking up. Peggy should have known Carole didn't need her protection. 'We all know your maths are rubbish! You, with your subnormal intellect. Coming into Baz's home and trying to steal her dog.'

'What?' Mitch blinked before turning back to face Peggy. 'Don't even try to pretend you don't know what I'm talking about. She's not—'

'Get to the point,' Peggy hissed between gritted teeth.

Across the room, Baz hugged Truffles closer to herself.

Mitch closed his eyes and took two deep breaths. When he opened them again, he continued. 'I'm turning the tables on you lot. You old bats thought you could beat me at my own game. But I've been at this a *long* time.'

With a melodramatic sigh, Peggy replied, 'You may have been at this – whatever *this* is – for a long time, but I'm a lot older than you, young man. If you don't come to the point in the next few seconds, I'm likely to expire right here on your sofa.'

'What I have here is evidence.' He held up one of the folders in his hands as he grinned at each woman in turn –

though Peggy noticed he skipped over Carole. 'Evidence showing that you ladies are behind the frauds. In fact, it looks as though you set the whole thing up in order to make yourselves out to be the heroes.' He paused – a smarmy grin on his face.

It was clear he thought he'd bested them. 'Just like you tried to make everyone think you solved the mysterious case of the Killer Queen—'

'The Rainbow Ripper,' Baz clarified.

'What?'

When he turned his gaze on her, Baz appeared to deflate. 'Never mind,' she squeaked. Peggy hated the thought of anyone ever making her friend feel that small.

'Whatever.' Mitch shook his head – the grin never sliding off his face. 'My point is, you wanted everyone to think you solved the case but you didn't actually do anything. You "investigated".' Peggy could hear the air quotes he put around the word. 'But you didn't *achieve* anything. If that fellow hadn't had a heart attack while burying his latest victim, he'd have gone right on killing.'

Peggy exchanged a sly glance with Madge.

'My point is, you ladies are nothing.' He was enjoying this. He thought he'd bested them. 'You're nosy and you meddle in other people's affairs. But all you create is trouble. And this time, you messed with the wrong man.'

Peggy allowed a small chuckle to escape her lips. 'Did we?'

Mitch patted the folder on his lap. 'The tables have turned, ladies. I've got all the evidence right here. It shows that *you* are behind the romance fraud. I'm not above sending it to the police.' He gave a small smile. 'Of course, we don't *have* to do that. You could just give me back the properties you stole from me. Oh, and that café of yours, naturally.'

Ah, so that was his plan, was it? Turning their own techniques back on them – using what he knew to blackmail them into actions they didn't want to take.

'We didn't—' Baz's voice cracked.

Mitch cocked his head. 'Oh, come now. The prices you made me sell at were a steal. But they were nothing compared to the prices you're going to sell them back to me at. Because you're not going to sell th—'

'You're darn right I'm not.' Baz hugged the dog so tightly to herself that Peggy was starting to worry she might squish the poor creature.

'No, I mean, you're going to *give* me the properties. And the business.' He opened a second folder on his lap and removed a stack of papers. 'I've got all the documents drawn up. All you need to do is sign them.'

Peggy scoffed. 'We're not going to do that!'

Mitch shrugged. 'Then I think we're done here.' He stood up and took several steps forwards. 'The police will—'

But he didn't get any further than that because Carole moved like lightning. Peggy hadn't even seen her retrieve the wooden rolling pin from her bag. Carole stepped right up to him, face to face. In a flash – before he could so much as blink in response – her rolling pin flew into his throat. One strike from Carole and he went down like a sack of bricks. She bent down and added a second strike, this time to his forehead.

They'd chosen the weapon carefully. It had to be the right shape and the right material for their plan to work.

Carole grinned broadly as she waved the rolling pin around gleefully. 'Still got it.' Small droplets of blood flew across the room, hitting the wall next to the fireplace. Peggy would need to remember to wipe that up before leaving.

Baz got to her feet, still clutching the dog to her chest. 'Two hits?' Peggy heard her breath catching in her throat. 'One hit to take him down and a second to ... to ... to finish the job? That's all it took? He can't possibly be dead.'

Madge was kneeling on the floor next to him, stethoscope in hand. 'He's gone.'

'What? Are you sure?' Baz stroked Truffle's fur in a way that Peggy suspected did far more for Baz than it did for the dog.

'Hangman's fracture.' Carole used a handkerchief to wipe down her rolling pin. 'Hyperextension of the pars interarticularis of C2. So named because it's the—'

Baz somehow managed to raise her hands to forestall any additional description from Carole without letting go of the dog. 'Thank you. I get it.'

'Good.' Carole slid the rolling pin back into her handbag.

But Madge held out her hand. 'Give me that. We're going to need to add some strategic bruising along his legs in order to make this look believable.' She paused. 'Please.'

Carole handed the rolling pin over to Madge, who used it to wave in the direction of the back garden. 'You two take the dog through to the kitchen. Carole and I will manage things in here.'

Peggy looked around at all the tea things. 'Baz, you go on into the kitchen and sit yourself down. You look like you're going to collapse. I'll join you in a sec.'

Baz nodded and left the room. Peggy gathered up the empty plates and stacked a couple of mugs atop them. She carried them through to the kitchen. Baz had closed the door but Peggy managed to elbow the handle into opening for her. She set the stack down on the counter and then returned for the remaining mugs and the cutlery.

When Peggy returned to the living room, Madge was using the rolling pin to apply judicious thwacks to the corpse's legs. Once she was satisfied with her work, she handed the rolling pin back to Carole.

Peggy carried the remaining dishes through to the kitchen, where she found Baz loading the plates into the dishwasher. 'I thought we were going to do those by hand.'

Baz, who was still trembling ever so slightly, looked up at her. 'Oh, right. I forgot.'

Her voice sounded off to Peggy's ears. She looked into the dishwasher. 'Well, it's almost full. No harm done. Once we add these, it'll be ready to set off.'

Baz was still standing in front of the dishwasher, holding the same plate she'd been holding when Peggy had walked into the room.

Peggy waved a hand towards the table. 'Why don't you take a seat, dear? I can finish up here. You look like you could do with a cuppa.'

Baz collapsed into the nearest chair. Truffles leapt straight back into her lap. 'Shouldn't we be helping Madge and Carole?'

Peggy struggled with the teapot, trying to figure out how to position it in the dishwasher. 'Their tasks are physically demanding. We'd only get in their way. Our responsibilities are in here, making it look as though Mitch cleaned up after our visit.'

After a minute, Baz walked back over and took the teapot out of her hands, swapping it for the small dog. 'Let me do that. You're making a hash of it, Peggy.'

Peggy stroked the dog's silky fur. 'Sorry, I've never had a dishwasher. Can't quite get the hang of the blasted things.'

'But surely your parents—'

Peggy barked out a laugh. 'My parents had *people*.'

'Ah.' Baz leant against the counter and took a slow breath, seeming to regain her strength.

Once the dishwasher was all loaded, Baz swiftly located the tablets and set the machine off on a cycle. Together, the two women set about tidying the kitchen up. They didn't need to remove their fingerprints from everything – it would be apparent the four women had visited. But they did remove them from places it wouldn't be normal for guests to touch.

As they worked, Truffles pottered about their feet.

Peggy looked around herself. 'This really is a lovely big kitchen.'

Baz pushed the dining chair back under the table before looking up. 'Is it? I hadn't considered. I suppose you're right. That garden, though' – she waved a hand towards the folding doors on the far side of the room – 'is absolutely lovely. Small but perfect.'

Peggy walked to the doors and looked through. 'Mizzle.'

Baz scooped the dog up into her arms and walked over to join her. 'What's that?'

Peggy motioned at the outdoor space. 'The weather. It's mizzling.'

'Drizzling, you mean?'

The pair stood side by side looking out at the small garden.

'Mizzle,' Peggy repeated. 'It's a misty drizzle.' She raised a hand and pointed once more. 'What's that steep embankment beyond the back wall?'

Baz pursed her lips and raised her eyebrows for just a second before answering. 'That's the nature reserve.'

A grin spread across Peggy's face. 'Is it really? I'm glad we were able to save it from redevelopment.' She waved a hand in the air. 'You know, so to speak.'

As Baz nodded, Madge pushed open the kitchen door. 'You two finished in here?'

'Sorry, Madge.' Baz's face flushed a delicate pink. 'We weren't—'

Peggy cut her unnecessary apology off. 'We only just finished a minute ago. Then we took a moment to admire the view of the nature reserve.'

Madge nodded. 'Good work. We're finished out front. It's time to get going.'

They joined the others at the front of the house, where they found Mitch posed face-down at the bottom of the stairs, his booted leg splayed awkwardly. To all appearances, it looked as though he'd fallen and landed badly.

Peggy walked over to the spot of blood on the wall. 'We need to clear this up.'

Madge walked up beside her. 'Good eye.' She pulled an antimicrobial wipe from her handbag and removed the incriminating evidence. Once she was finished, she deposited the used wipe into a plastic bag inside her handbag.

Peggy couldn't help but notice Baz averting her eyes from the corpse as she rummaged through drawers and cupboards. 'I can't find his harness and lead.'

'For heaven's sake, Baz.' Peggy shook her head. 'You'd have an easier time of it if you put the dog down while you look.'

'I can't.' Baz scrunched up her face as though she were struggling not to cry. 'He shouldn't have to see his ... his ... his master ... like that.'

Madge stood up from where she'd been putting her shoes on. She put a hand on Baz's arm. 'Pass him to me.' She took the dog in one arm and gently patted Baz's shoulder. Peggy helped Baz in her search while Madge fussed over the tiny dog.

But it was Carole who found the harness and lead. 'They were in the downstairs loo.'

Soon they were all on their way. Madge pulled the door to behind herself, still holding Truffles in one arm.

Baz opened her umbrella before setting her handbag in her scooter's basket. 'Are you all right walking Truffles, Madge? If not, maybe once I get myself in position, you can—'

'I'll be fine.' Madge set the small dog on the ground and

then opened her own brolly. She looked around to make sure everyone was ready to go.

The four women returned the way they'd come, following the footpath through Brookmill Park to Baz's flat.

Once they were inside, Baz asked Madge to fix everyone a cup of tea while she attended to Truffles. The poor dog looked like a drowned rat. Peggy joined Carole on the sofa. Once he'd been towelled off, Truffles – seemingly unaware that his little life had changed forever – hopped up and settled himself into the tiny space between the pair. Peggy rested a hand on him.

When Baz handed her a mug of coffee, Peggy thanked her. 'Daisy knows she's meant to be walking this little lad tonight?'

'Oh, she's over the moon about it.' Baz settled herself onto the opposite sofa. 'I told her I had a friend who'd broken his foot and his little dog needed some extra walking. She's delighted at the thought of having a dog around the place for a few hours.'

Peggy stroked the creature's silky fur. 'And how will you explain that he's here all night?' They'd been through this in the planning phase, of course. But Peggy wanted to be sure Baz was keeping her wits about her.

Baz crossed her legs and took a sip of the tea. 'I've told her he's out this evening and he'll ring me when he's back. When it's time for bed and we've had no contact, I'll tell her that we may as well leave it until the morning.'

Peggy touched her tongue to the roof of her mouth a few times. 'Maybe give her some indication that he might be quite late, and if so, you agreed you'd bring the dog back in the morning.'

The steam from Madge's tea fogged her glasses as she took a long drink. 'That's not a bad idea, Peggy. We wouldn't want Daisy to stay awake all night, thinking he's going to ring at any moment.'

Baz set her mug down on a coaster on the coffee table. 'That's a good idea.' Peggy couldn't abide coasters. *Why bother? If your furniture isn't made to be used, what's the point of it?*

As soon as the beverages had been drunk and bladders had been emptied, it was time for the women to make their way home.

Just before they left, Madge squeezed Baz's shoulder. 'You did well today.'

Baz frowned. 'I didn't do anything, though. I feel so useless, so—'

'Stop.' Madge wagged a finger. 'Without you, we'd never have worked out who was behind the scheme. We all play our own roles. I'd be no good at what Carole does. Peggy would be no good at what I do.'

Peggy smiled as warmly as she could. 'We play to our strengths, not our weaknesses – that's what we have each other for.'

'Thank you.' Baz nodded. 'I'll see you for coffee in the morning.' She clutched the dog to her chest and planted a kiss on his head.

wherein decisions need to be made

BAZ STEERED her mobility scooter into the road, having made sure to check no one was turning south onto Brookmill Road first. Truffles walked neatly at her side. He'd taken to it like an old pro. She'd even put a little basket at her feet. Whenever he grew tired or if she needed to speed up, she'd pop him into the basket; he rode like a champ.

It had been almost three weeks since he'd joined her little family. Already, she couldn't imagine life without a dog. How she'd managed the last year and a half, she'd never know.

For his part, Truffles sometimes cried and searched the flat for his former master. When they were out walking, he occasionally tried to pull her towards his previous house.

Of course, Mitch hadn't called for Baz to return his dog that fateful night. After a few days, Madge and Baz had returned to his house one sunny afternoon. Peeking through the mail slot, Madge had rung the emergency services, telling them she could see what appeared to be a body.

They'd both been interviewed by the police several times. But the cops found nothing suspicious about his death. Since

Truffles seemed so comfortable in her care, they asked her if she'd be willing to look after him for a few days while they contacted Mitch's family.

But no one ever came to claim the dog—

She was pulled from her thoughts when someone called her name. 'Good morning, Ms Spencer. We should really stop meeting like this.'

Baz chuckled as she tried to catch her breath. 'Oh, Jerome! Sorry, I was miles away – almost didn't see you.'

'You should be more careful, auntie. I'd hate for you to get hurt.' Jerome used his hand to shield his eyes from the sun. 'How are you? Hopefully doing better than the last time we met.'

Baz reached down to settle Truffles, who was keen to keep walking. 'I'm well, thank you. How are you?'

'I'm good, thanks.' Jerome squatted down and held his hand out for Truffles, who licked it. 'And who's this little one? I don't remember you having a dog.'

'He's the newest member of my family,' Baz said proudly.

'Aw, that's good. He's a friendly little fellow. I'm sure he brightens up your day. You certainly seem happy.'

Baz smiled. They chatted for a few moments before they each continued on their respective way.

A minute later, she steered her mobility scooter into its usual spot between the public car park and the outdoor tables at Wellbeloved Café. 'Here we are.' She switched the engine off and dropped the key into her handbag.

As she was about to dismount the scooter, a cheerful voice startled her.

'Morning, banana!' Carole held out her elbow for Baz to take. Peggy stood beside her, her hand in Carole's other elbow and Cookie at her side.

Baz smiled as she accepted. 'Good morning, Ca—' But that

was as far as she got because the moment Truffles spied Cookie, he lunged and barked excitedly at him.

Cookie responded by reversing course and hiding behind Peggy.

Peggy turned around and coaxed Cookie back out into his usual space by her side. 'You silly boy. What's all this cowering and shaking about, eh? He's not going to hurt you. He weighs less than your front paw, you ridiculous creature.'

Carole tsked. 'Do not give what is holy to dogs, and do not throw your pearls before swine.'

Baz scooped her new dog up into her arms. 'I promise he's not trying to hurt Cookie – he just wants to play.'

'Oh, I can tell.' Peggy began moving again, walking towards the café's entrance. 'Believe me, I know. You think I'd let him threaten my boy?'

The bell sounded as Peggy pushed open the door. She and Carole headed straight into the main room while Baz went to the counter to place her order, Truffles still in her arms.

As Baz passed the archway between the rooms, she spied a certain man sitting next to Madge. She gave a little wave. Jimi had been coming into the café with Madge a couple mornings a week lately. In the year Baz had known Madge, she'd never known the other woman to stick with one man. But she'd been married – three and a half times, apparently – so she must do sometimes.

Baz walked up to the cash register – or whatever they called machines that didn't even accept cash.

'Morning, Ms Spencer,' said Sarah. 'How are you doing today? And how is your little dog?'

'I'm doing very well indeed. Thank you.' Baz couldn't help beaming, but then immediately she felt guilty. 'And Truffles is well too. Last night, we had final confirmation that he's mine now.'

Sarah entered Baz's order into the computer. 'Aw, that's excellent news. He seems really happy with you and Daisy.'

'He is. Thank you.' Baz tapped her phone to the device to pay for her tea. 'And how about you? Have you managed to get some help yet? You've been run off your feet since Olena left.'

Sarah visibly relaxed. 'I've got a new person starting next week. I'm looking forward to being able to breathe again.'

Baz nodded. 'I'll get out of your way. We'll come back over to collect our drinks in a few minutes.'

'Cheers, I'd appreciate that.'

Still holding the dog in her arms, Baz joined her friends. As soon as she rounded the corner into the second room, Truffles once again lunged and yapped at poor Cookie. Jimi stood up, stepping sharply away from Cookie – which made Baz giggle. Cookie wasn't the one misbehaving. That was Truffles, though people always made excuses for poor behaviour from small dogs.

Well, she certainly wasn't going to be that sort of dog-mother. She took Truffles' little snoot gently but firmly and told him 'No!' At least he wasn't being aggressive – that would have added another layer of awkwardness. 'You need to learn to take no for an answer. Cookie doesn't want to play with you.'

Madge kissed her teeth. 'Morning, Baz. Haven't you called my Tony yet? He'll help you get that dog under control in no time.' One of her sons ran a dog-training service, though Baz hadn't yet met him in person.

Peggy nodded. 'Indeed. He was a tremendous help with Cookie. Not that you can tell by the way he's behaving now.' The giant dog was, of course, hiding behind his mistress once again.

Jimi bent forwards and kissed Madge softly – taking care not to put his feet anywhere near Cookie. 'I'd best be going, my beautiful. Time to open my shop.' He looked at Baz. 'I'm committed to making it a success.'

'I have every confidence in you, Jimi,' Baz said, and she meant it. She'd helped him arrange sessions with a business coach to make sure his plan was viable. He'd hired a freelance social media manager for two hours a week to help him promote his business. And she'd agreed to accept a reduced rent for his first year to give him his best chance.

He doffed an imaginary cap at the women and bade them farewell.

Baz kept hold of Truffles as she took her seat. 'I have called Tony, actually. We've arranged to have our first session later this week.' She was looking forward to getting Truffles better socialised so he could be around other dogs without so much excitement. At the moment, she wasn't able to do any embroidery work at the café as she had to keep the dog on her lap.

Madge looked pleased. 'Good.'

Baz was bursting to tell the group her news. But first, Madge should have an update of her own. 'Didn't you say Chuk was planning to stop by yesterday evening? How did that go?'

'Thank you, Baz.' Madge nodded approvingly. 'The Home Office has responded to Marta and Reyn's applications. Now Chukwuma needs to prepare their evidence. He says he's confident the appeals will be successful.'

Baz felt so pleased for the pair.

'Chukwuma said he believes their original asylum claims were rejected for technical reasons,' Madge continued. 'Now that they have him overseeing things...' She waved a dismissive hand. 'They'd be successful even without everything that happened to them – poor kids.'

'I'm glad.' Baz hoped he was right. He was an expert, so presumably he knew what he was talking about. 'And I hope they find the person at the detention centre who...' She couldn't quite bring herself to say 'sold them'.

Madge kissed her teeth. 'Disgusting business. Chukwuma is gathering evidence on that as well. That person will see justice done.'

There was silence for a moment, before Madge looked up from her knitting. 'Now, tell us how *your* meeting with the lawyer went.'

Heat warmed Baz all the way through. 'Actually...'

Peggy closed her laptop and looked up. 'Now, that sounds promising.'

Madge looked at Peggy. 'I told you there had to be a reason she wanted to meet with Baz again. Didn't I say so?'

'Just make sure you don't agree to participate in any testing,' added Carole. 'They're forever looking for people to get involved with their experiments. It's all about trying to revive the Hittite race, you know.'

Sarah came in with a tray of teapots and mugs. The women chatted amiably for the minute it took her to distribute all the drinks.

Baz ran her fingers through her dog's silky fur. Two weeks before, she'd been contacted by Samantha, a lovely young woman who represented Mitch's estate, acting as his executor. They'd made an appointment for her to come to Baz's place to discuss Truffles.

At the time, Baz had assumed the meeting would culminate in having to pass the dog over. She'd been surprised by how much the idea pained her.

When Samantha arrived at her flat, they'd had a very nice chat. The young lawyer told her that Mitch had left specific instructions to ensure she found Truffles a good home. She said that various family members had been asked about taking the dog on, but they'd all declined.

Per the terms of Mitch's will, that left Samantha in the position of finding him a good home.

Baz had been shocked when, after just ten minutes, Samantha had asked her if she'd be interested in keeping Truffles permanently.

Baz had almost burst into tears right then and there. *Of course I'll keep him! I don't want to imagine life without him.*

And then a few days later, Samantha had rung again. She said they'd need to have another meeting. That had taken place yesterday afternoon.

'I had thought yesterday's appointment was purely for the purpose of signing the adoption papers.' Baz hugged Truffles to herself.

Peggy made a rolling motion. 'Yes, and? I take it there was more to it than just that ritual.'

Baz swallowed. 'It was about Mitch's will.'

Madge peered over the top of her glasses at Baz. 'His will?'

Peggy cackled. 'Well, there's no way in hell he left you anything. I mean, can you even imagine?'

Baz had to wait for Peggy and Madge to stop hooting with laughter. 'Well, actually...'

'No!' Peggy's eyebrows were sky-high.

Even Madge stopped her knitting, her hands uncharacteristically still. 'He never!'

Peggy wagged a finger. 'It won't be anything you want – that's for certain.'

Baz bobbled her head. 'He didn't leave anything to me, per se. Well, he did but—'

Peggy flapped both her hands impatiently. 'Spit it out already!'

Baz repositioned the dog on her lap. 'The lawyer, she ... well, she had her instructions, you see. She asked Mitch's nephew whether he'd be willing to take Truffles. But he declined. So then she asked all his other family members. Most of them told her to send him to a shelter.'

She clutched him tight to her chest. 'I mean, can you even imagine? His sister suggested that they put him down.' She wiped a tear from her eye. 'I can't even bear to think of it.'

'You already knew you were allowed to keep him.' Peggy shook her head. 'This isn't news.'

'Samantha told me that – even in our first meeting – she could see what a bond he and I had. She said she was so pleased that I'd been willing to keep him. And then she said—' Baz pressed her fingers to her lips. She still couldn't quite believe what she was about to say.

'Oh, get to the point already, would you?' Peggy looked like she wanted to throw something at Baz. 'I am very old, you know – it would be nice if you could get to the point before I expire.'

Baz wiped another tear from her eye. 'The bulk of Mitch's estate went to his nephew. But his house – the one we visited – it goes to Truffles.'

Madge blinked. 'He willed his house to the *dog*?'

'Yes, no, sort of.' Baz struggled to put the words together. 'The terms of his will said that the executor – that's Samantha – had to offer the dog first to the nephew. If he wouldn't take him in, then she had to try other family members. And if none of them would take him – or if she deemed them unsuitable – then she had the task of finding him a good home. And she was expressly forbidden from telling anyone that there was any bequest accompanying him.'

Samantha had smiled so broadly when she told Baz this.

'Whoever adopts Truffles also gets the house,' Baz said. 'Plus a very generous monthly stipend for the rest of his life.'

Peggy startled both dogs when she gave a thunderous clap. Truffles buried himself deeper into Baz's armpit.

Then Peggy made one of her trademarked sceptical faces. 'And yet no one in the family wanted him? That's fishy.'

Madge nodded. 'Very fishy.'

Baz raised her hands. 'That's what I'm trying to tell you. Samantha was under orders not to let anyone know about the conditional elements of the bequests until after the question of Truffles had been settled to her satisfaction. Apparently Mitch chose to work with her specifically because she's an animal lover. He trusted her to do right by this little fellow.'

'Huh.' Peggy opened her laptop back up. 'So he was only a *mostly* terrible human after all.'

Madge studied Baz. 'Well, what are you going to do?'

Baz frowned. 'How do you mean? I'm going to keep Truffles, of course! And I'll reimburse all Mitch's victims. And I thought I might buy Big Joe a mobility scooter so he can gad about the neighbourhood a bit.'

Madge shook her head. 'Of course. We never doubted you'd keep the dog.'

Peggy grinned approvingly. 'And reimbursing his victims is the right thing to do.'

'And Big Joe will appreciate being able to get out and about,' Madge said.

'I'm hoping Cheryl can help me put things right,' Baz said. 'Anonymously, of course.'

'I'm sure she'd be very pleased,' Madge said. 'But I meant about the house. Will you continue living in the flat or move in?'

'Or you could sell them both and move somewhere even more grand,' added Peggy.

'What?' Baz leant forwards and poured some tea into her mug. 'But this isn't just about me! This is for all of us to discuss and decide.'

'Why?' Peggy shrugged. 'We're not adopting Truffles – you are.'

Adding a splash of oat milk to her tea, Baz said, 'Because it's not fair that I keep getting richer off—' She couldn't quite figure out how to finish that sentence without mentioning the group's criminal activities, so she just moved on. 'While you three, you know, don't. Why don't one of you take the house? Or I could move into the house and you could take my flat – it's bigger than ... well, than either of yours.'

Madge and Peggy exchanged a look.

Peggy shook her head. 'Both my family and Carole's keep offering to move us into some place "better".' Peggy's flaked black nail polish showed as she made rabbit ears around the relevant word. 'I refuse to take handouts from them and I'm certainly not taking one from you.'

'I've lived in my flat for almost fifty years,' said Madge. 'They'll be carrying my corpse out of there at some point.' She raised a hand. 'Not for a good many years yet, mind.'

Baz's shoulders fell. 'Well, what am I supposed to do, then?'

Peggy picked up her espresso and knocked it back in a single swallow. 'I'd be perfectly happy to serve as a sounding board for your ideas. But only you can decide what's right for you. Well, and your granddaughter, of course. Since it affects her too.'

Madge gave a sly grin. 'And I bet your young man might like to have a say in it as well.'

Baz felt her skin warm at the thought of Paul. He did deserve to have a say in what she did next, didn't he? 'I suppose it might be nice to live in a house with a garden.'

Carole began to sing the opening lines of Garbage's 'Only Happy When It Rains'.

Madge opened her eyes wide and wagged a finger in Carole's direction. 'Oh, now there's an idea.'

Peggy grinned as she placed a hand on Carole's knee. 'That's an excellent suggestion, my love.'

The implications of Carole's surreal speech pattern filtered through Baz's brain and she realised what Carole was implying. 'Oh!' She turned to Madge. 'But won't you miss having them around? You've been so much happier since they moved in.'

Madge waved her knitting with a flourish. 'Don't worry about me. It won't be long before the charity sends me new guests. I've already had to turn them away once last week.'

Baz's heart soared as she considered it. 'I'll give it some thought. And then I'll offer whichever property I don't need to Reyn and Marta. That's a brilliant solution. Thank you, Carole.'

Carole looked her in the eye. 'It was just a story, you know. It was never really about Napoleon.'

'What will you do about the stairs?' Madge's glasses fogged over as she poured herself a cup of scalding-hot red tea. 'If you decide to take the house, that is.'

'Hmm.' Baz frowned. Her knee had improved a lot over the two years since the accident but she didn't think she could tolerate going up and down the stairs all the time.

'It's a shame it doesn't have a downstairs bathroom,' mused Peggy.

'It has a loo on the main level, though.' Madge sat back and resumed her knitting. 'It would be easy enough to add a shower. You'd lose a bit of space in the dining room, though.'

Peggy looked at Madge. 'But then what would she do with the whole upstairs of the place?'

An idea occurred to Baz. 'I suppose Daisy's going to need space of her own at some point. Maybe we could sort of split the house into two flats.'

'That could work,' said Peggy and Madge at the same time.

'I'll need to discuss it with Daisy.' Baz nodded to herself. 'And Paul, too, of course.'

the end (for now)

Thank you for reading *A Bit of Murder Between Friends*, the third novel in the *Vigilauntie Justice* series. Baz, Peggy, Carole, and Madge will almost certainly continue their mission to keep south-east London safe in future stories.

Sign up to my newsletter to get updates on what I'm working on, top-secret discounts, dog pics, and free stories.

Click the image above to get Friends in Need for free

acknowledgements

I keep seeing posts in various writers and readers groups saying that writers shouldn't get political in their novels.

But everything is politics. Everything.

Governments all over the world are oppressing people for who they are, who they love, how they express themselves, where they were born, the colour of their skin, their religion ... and for having the audacity to live as their authentic selves. To remain neutral is to side with the oppressor.

Thank you for reading.

J.M. Redmann provided some early input on this book. She very gently reminded me of writing advice I thought I'd already taken to heart – but had actually forgotten.

As always, the WiFi Sci-Fi writers' group has been the most amazing gift. They continually teach, push, and cheerlead me to be a better writer.

I want to thank my beta readers: Isabelle Felix and Nick Taylor. They both got stuck right into the guts of my ridiculous tale and helped provide a buff and polish.

Hannah McCall, my editor, dug into the meat of this vegetarian story to make it the best version of itself it could be. Any mistakes you find now are entirely my own fault.

Finally, my legally contracted lifemate, Dave, has been putting up with more than any human being should have to. If you've ever met me in real life, you'll understand what a big deal that is. Seriously ... I'm *a lot*. Dave has listened to me talk about my imaginary friends every single day for seven and a half years. Dave's the best person.

ELLIOTT HAY (two Ts and any pronouns) dreams of a world where nice little old ladies don't have to <ahem> take matters into their own hands.

In real life, they're a Canadian misanthrope who lives in Deptford, *sarf ees* London. They share their home with their partner and an assortment of waifs and strays. When not writing convoluted, inefficient stories, she spends her time telling financial services firms to behave more efficiently. When not doing either of those things, they can be found in the pub or shouting at people online – occasionally practising efficiency by doing both at once.

As someone who's neurodivergent, an immigrant, and the

proud owner of an invisible disability, she strives to present a realistically diverse array of characters in her stories.

They also write sci-fi (without the pew-pew) under the name Si Clarke.

www.ingramcontent.com/pod-product-compliance
Lightning Source LLC
Chambersburg PA
CBHW011558190726
48287CB00010B/2960